NIGHT LIGHT

AND OTHER STORIES

By

Jerry Garces

DeeBee

Contents

Dedication

To John and Belia, my parents and members of the Greatest Generation.

A WAR STORY

"WHAT MAKES YOU THINK THEY STOLE YOUR SCREENPLAY?

Late afternoon sun streamed through the dusty windows and splashed across the office walls as Ron Montgomery, arms folded across his chest, posed the question to a potential client. Ed Scott chewed his lip and ran his fingers through his thick gray hair. He swore that the latest box office megahit was ripped off from a script he'd written three years earlier. Getting someone to believe him proved more of a challenge than he'd anticipated.

Ron had nearly canceled the consultation altogether, but changed his mind, thinking it would be an interesting diversion from a slow and dreary week. His small, non-descript law office sat across the street from one of the older movie theaters in town, its antique two-sided overhead marquee pointing streetward. The tired office offered just enough space within its cheap, faded, paneled walls for a bookcase, a wooden desk, and printer, along with assorted certificates on the wall. Not exactly the kind of lawyer's office he envisioned as a young, ambitious student back in the day, but he'd resigned himself to his lot in life.

"That movie, *A Soldiers' Camp*, is the story I wrote!" Ed straightened his back and leaned forward in his chair. A bead of sweat formed across his forehead. "I sent a copy of the screenplay to Lon Dominic at Global Pictures as an entry in their contest. I knew that if I got a filmmaker to read it, man, it would sell!" Ed couldn't sit still, talking with his hands, occasionally running his fingers through his hair. "Someone later told me that it never arrived—that it must have been lost. Then, one day this movie appears and it's my story. It's the one I sent in to those bastards."

Ron narrowed his gaze and studied his potential client. He knew that most people don't give up the whole story—not at first anyway—and wondered what this Ed fellow wasn't telling him.

"Do you have anything to prove that you sent the screenplay to Global? Maybe a courier's receipt or something?" Ron would not let Ed get away without a yes or no on this one.

Ed smiled as he reached into a worn leather briefcase next to his chair. He brought out an old, faded, postal return receipt requested card sent to Global Pictures. It bore an illegible signature. "This is it," he said, handing it to Ron. "I waited a month for a response. I called. That's when they said they never got it."

Ron looked over the card which was in very poor condition. "Okay, so what was your story about?" If he took the case, he'd have to brush up on copyright law.

"Have you seen *A Soldiers' Camp*?"

"No," Ron said as he rubbed his square jaw, then adjusted his glasses. He didn't get out much since his wife left.

She thought he should have been a more successful lawyer. She left and moved in with a judge, leaving Ron in their small apartment. They had no children which made the split easier. At 31 years of age, some days he felt tired and used up.

"The movie is the same as my story. A Mexican–American named Frank Chavez from East Los Angeles joins the army before Pearl Harbor. In training, he's such a good shot they send him to sniper school. During the war, he's captured in France, but not executed. The Germans shot snipers on the spot, ya know." Ed had done some research. "A German soldier with a conscience saves Frank's life. Frank goes to a Stalag where the camp commandant, Hoffman, finds out Frank was a sniper." Ron's face remained expressionless. "Hoffman does not have Frank executed because he learns that Frank speaks Spanish. Are you with me?"

"Yes, so is that what the movie is about?" Ron would have to see the script—if Ed had one.

"Okay! Frank and the Commandant save each other's lives because they both speak Spanish. There are private meetings where Hoffman sharpens his Spanish speaking ability and Frank begins to understand Hoffman. In the end, when the camp is liberated, they both escape to places where Spanish is spoken. Frank returns to post-war East Los Angeles and Hoffman manages to get to South America. Then there's all the conflict that takes the audience to another level, man against man, man against himself, all that jazz. I did my share of research for the script."

Ron thought a moment, then said, "So, do you have a copy of the script?" This story was getting interesting; Ron's eyes brightened.

From the leather briefcase, Ed drew a nearly two-inch-thick manuscript. "Right here. It's the only copy I have. Please read it, Mr. Montgomery. It will prove that Global stole my story!"

"I'm hesitant to take it if it's the only one there is." Ron still did not know whether he would take the case.

"Go ahead, I trust you." Ed now seemed overly cheerful.

Ron grabbed the manuscript. The cover read *Friendly Enemies*.

"Read it, then see the movie. If you don't agree they're the same, I'll take it back and never darken your doorstep again." Ed's eyes sparkled as he stood and straightened his corduroy coat.

"Fair enough, Mr. Scott." Ron inhaled deeply. "Today is Thursday. I'll give you a call Monday afternoon and tell you what I think." Ron got up from his desk to lead Ed to the door. Ten minutes after Ed had disappeared, Ron began reading.

Ron was a sole practitioner. He had been in the law business in Arizona for four years after receiving his law degree from a correspondence school in Iowa. After the grand opening of his office, he learned that people don't call for advice every day and bring wheelbarrows full of cash to the door. It took time and money just to set up a practice. He kept the overhead low by utilizing the local law library, signing on with a phone answering service and having his typing done by family law paralegals who had an office in the building next door. Ron's budget didn't allow for malpractice insurance.

At times, he was glad that his wife, Angie, had left him. She wanted to be the rich wife of a rich lawyer. They were first attracted to each other's good looks. He was taking courses in law when they met, and they married just five months after being introduced. When she realized what it took to earn a living in the law business, along with the sacrifices, she found an exit from their marriage by marrying a judge. "A judge has a good secure income," Angie said at the time, "and doesn't have to beat the bushes for clients."

The screenplay proved very interesting. Ron thought the characters and the details made the story come alive. He wondered about the part during World War II in the United States, where people were unable to buy butter, sugar, gasoline and tires without government coupons. *What a time that must have been*, he thought.

At around 7:30 in the evening, he finished reading. He got up, stretched, and said to himself, "Well, I guess I'll be going to the movies tonight." He planned to grab a hot dog for dinner on the way. He wasn't in the habit of eating well since Angie left.

After the show, Ron drifted into Stockman's Bar for a drink. He was amazed at the similarities between *A Soldiers' Camp* and *Friendly Enemies*. Overall, the stories were the same—an American POW meets a German commander who spent time in New York City before the war. They both speak Spanish and the POW tutors the German at his request. Two other identical points struck in Ron's mind. These were the posting of guards to keep prisoners from eating out of garbage cans, and injuries to prisoners from biting into bread baked with thumbtacks or glass inside. The bread was baked in a nearby town by civilians who believed in a duty to inflict pain on those who dared invade the Fatherland. It looked like a clear case of a "screenplay theft" as he thought of it. But he would need help in this copyright case against Global Productions.

His friend and colleague, Benson Bragg, had the proper resources. Ron would have to offer Ben a large percentage of any recovery in exchange for the needed help. The two had been close since working a civil rights action against the police department a year earlier. Ron's share of that settlement was enough to buy two cars: one for himself, and one for Angie. Wasting no time, Angie spent the remaining cash on clothes and jewelry before leaving.

Ron called Ben the next morning. "How's the law business, Ben?"

"Could be better. What's up?" Ben had just settled for $600,000 with an insurance company over a product liability case. These were the kind of settlements that kept him in a spacious office in one of the best office buildings in Phoenix.

"I've got something for us!"

"So, who's got the deep pocket?" Ben said, as he stroked his mustache flanked by puffy cheeks. Before any investigation or legal work could start, Ben needed to know up front whether the potential defendant in a civil case had money enough to make a case worthwhile.

"Global Pictures and producer Lon Dominic." Ron waited for Ben's response. When none came, he reiterated, "I said—"

"I heard what you said. Are you serious?"

"Let's get together and talk about it, Ben. I have the screenplay upon which the film *A Soldiers' Camp* is based— the real screenplay!" Ron drew in a long breath. "Can we meet this week?"

"Why don't you come over tomorrow afternoon and we can talk about it." Phoenix was about a half hour drive from Ron's office in Mesa.

"Okay, see you at 2:30!" Ron had no appointments scheduled. He planned to do some research and bring the screenplay with him.

★ ★ ★

THE FOLLOWING DAY, ON ARRIVAL AT BEN'S LAW FIRM, Ron was greeted by a receptionist who led him into Ben's large office. The ornate room had white walls and a faux fireplace—a stark contrast to his own modest office.

Ben was known for high dollar settlements and court judgments. When he entered, the two greeted each other like brothers. Ben called for some iced tea, then they settled in to discuss Ron's previous meeting with Ed Scott, the screenplay, and the movie, *A Soldiers' Camp*.

Ben's mind raced as Ron outlined all the similarities between the screenplay and the movie. He leaned forward on his desk. He was very interested in joining Ron in a lawsuit against Global Pictures, and since *A Soldiers' Camp* had already grossed $55 million, the smell of cash overwhelmed him. He needed no other convincing.

Ed was thrilled when Ron called him and said that he would take the case and had secured the help of a legal rainmaker to assist. Within a month, they served Global with a complaint alleging copyright infringement, appropriation of intellectual property, and fraud.

Global's lawyers rejected the accusations and responded with a motion to move the case to New York City. Ron and Ben filed an opposition to the motion arguing that it would be a hardship for potential witnesses to travel out of state. The case hit the media and began generating publicity. Entertainment magazines followed the case and personalities involved. Finally, a judge determined to hear the case in California. The stakes grew. If Ron and Ben won, they could look forward to the notoriety that went with it—not to mention the settlement money. The case was worth millions in advertising alone.

Preparation for the trial included taking the depositions of producer Lon Domenic and employees at Global. Lon wasn't the type of man to hide from lawyers or anyone else. He stated plainly that if Ed Scott thought he could extort money from his company, he had another thing coming. Any similarities between the movie and Ed Scott's script had nothing to do with stealing any story ideas. Rick Ramirez, a Global screenwriter, testified at deposition that he never took anything from anyone. He resented any accusation that he stole anything. He felt so insulted that at one point he got up and left his deposition in anger. It was a full hour before his lawyers coaxed him into returning.

Six months dragged on without any offer of settlement from Global. Ron and Ben needed clear and convincing evidence that Scott's script had reached Global and was used in making *A Soldiers' Camp*. Ron had subpoenaed many documents, including mail logs for the time that Scott had sent the screenplay to Global. After a long court paper fight, Global's lawyers finally turned over the logs, but there was nothing in them to prove that Ed Scott's screenplay had been received and signed for.

As the trial date loomed, Ron and Ben knew it would be a tough sell to get a jury to believe that Scott's screenplay had been stolen to make the movie.

The first day of trial, Ron made his opening statement telling the jury that Ed Scott was an unpretentious, down to earth guy who worked hard on a screenplay only to have it stolen by a movie company that covered up the theft. He wanted to paint the trial as a David versus Goliath type of story to gain sympathy for his client.

Global's lawyers, meanwhile, painted "the dishonest Mr. Scott" as a no-talent hack writer of radio commercials and greeting cards. They spoke extensively of the company's background and track record in the business. Global, they said, was an entertainment company with high ethical standards and did not engage in fraud. Global didn't need to steal anything as they could hire the best writers in show business.

As the trial proceeded, Ben pinned his hopes on his investigator tracking down a secretary who worked at Global and who would have signed a log showing receipt of Scott's screenplay. A lot of money had gone into the case and neither Ron nor Ben could afford to quit looking for someone who could provide winning evidence beyond a scribbled signature on a postal receipt. They both hoped to find this woman before they ran out of cash.

At 4:00 p.m. on the third day of trial, Ben received a call from his investigator, a former cop.

"Mr. Bragg, this is Hubbard. I have news." He flicked ashes from his cigarette. "I found her."

"You have a former employee?" Ben hoped this was the right person. He paused, and took a breath. "Where was she?"

"At an AA meeting."

Ben paused. "What kind of shape is she in?"

"She's okay. Just didn't want to talk much," Hubbard said. "She'll meet with us if we don't take too much of her time."

"Okay, this evening at the hotel." Ben was concerned that she might lack credibility based on her being an alcoholic and possibly her physical condition if she was still recovering.

Martha Bain entered the hotel lobby and gazed around. Hubbard waved her over. She was tall, thin, and well-groomed. A pretty, red-haired woman in her late 40s, who they learned had tried her hand at acting once. She explained that she took the job as a secretary at Global hoping to somehow break into show business, but was never taken seriously and resented it. Martha had heard about the lawsuit against Global but did not care to get involved. She confirmed that it was her signature on the tattered return requested receipt form.

Martha spoke about a company executive who was always hitting on her and who had removed the mail log from her desk one afternoon. The next day, she had to keep bugging him to get it back. He returned it to her a week later, and said that if anyone asked, he had never taken the log. He was a heavy drinker and, not long after the log business, died in an auto accident after leaving a party.

They agreed that Martha Bain would testify the next day.

★ ★ ★

JUDGE ROY ENTERED HIS COURTROOM THE FOLLOWING morning. The bailiff called everyone to order. "All rise. Superior Court in and for the County of Los Angeles is now in order."

"Be seated," Roy said as he sat in his tall black leather chair behind the bench. He adjusted his robe and surveyed the room. "Alright, what's on in this case for today?"

Ron stood. "Your honor, we have located a key witness whose testimony we believe can show that the screenplay sent by Mr. Scott to Global Pictures did arrive and that it was read by at least one company executive." Global's lawyers shifted awkwardly on their chairs, looks of concern spreading across their faces.

Global's lead counsel stood up immediately. "Objection, your honor. Mr. Montgomery hasn't shown that this person is on their list of witnesses served on us and filed with the court. We have no advance notice. It is entirely prejudicial and completely unfair."

"We located Martha Bain yesterday, your honor," Ron said. "Opposing counsel will be able to cross examine. There should be no prejudice." Ron played a hunch that Judge Roy would allow Martha's testimony.

The judge cleared his throat. "Well, Mr. Montgomery, this calls for an offer of proof." Judge Roy was a fair man, liberal in allowing newly discovered evidence. Ron would have to explain Martha's proposed testimony to the court. He did so in a compelling manner.

Judge Roy listened and agreed that Martha could testify. Global lawyers asked for a recess until the following day, and the judge agreed.

Back at the hotel, Ron, Ben and Ed Scott gathered to discuss the morning's events.

"I think they would like to settle," Ben said, reading a note that the concierge handed him. Ron and Ed listened intently as Ben continued. "They want to meet before court in the morning.

"How much should we demand?" Ed could see nothing but dollar signs as he rubbed his hands together.

"Let's wait until we hear what they have to say," Ben said. "It would be premature to set any dollar amount now. We'll get some rest and see what happens in the morning."

In the early morning, Global presented its offer in a court hallway. "We think that under the present circumstances, $150,000 is a fair amount. Of course, the settlement would be confidential and Global would admit no liability." All three of

Global's lawyers were present. They smiled slightly and waited for a response.

"That's bull!" Scott yelled. "You guys have made millions off my story!"

"Hey! Let's keep this civil," countered Ben. "We don't have to take it." He looked toward Ron and Ed. "We are not interested."

"Listen, the offer is no good once we enter the courtroom," Global's lead counsel whispered. No one said a word. "Okay, see you in court." The three turned and walked away.

Martha testified before Judge Roy and the jury. With all the emotion of one seeking justice and nothing for herself, she gave her greatest performance. She never faltered on cross-examination and Judge Roy sanctioned Global's attorneys for trying to bring up Martha's alcoholism. He told the jurors it had no bearing on the case.

After six hours of deliberation, the jury brought in a verdict for Ed Scott. General damages of one million dollars. Punitive damages of twenty million. Ed jumped from his seat, "Hallelujah!"

Judge Roy banged his gavel as he ordered Ed to sit and stay quiet.

Outside the courthouse, Ron and Ben gave their victory speeches before microphones to a group of reporters. Ron had decided that now was the time to quit the law business and open a fancy restaurant. Ben talked of opening new offices in Los Angeles and Denver.

Ron, Ben, and Ed—along with Martha—all went to the hotel to celebrate. They sat in the lounge late in the afternoon. A large television was on over the bar. They arrived in time to see their victory reported on the local news. Within a half hour, a reporter came on to update the story. Global had filed for bankruptcy, and Lon Dominic had been taken to a hospital with some unknown ailment. The four were absolutely stunned.

"What happens now?" Ed asked, his face drained of color.

Ben stood up. "Me and Ron gotta talk to the other attorneys. We'll call you." The two left to make some phone calls. Later, they discovered that the bankruptcy was filed immediately after the jury's decision. An automatic stay was in effect. No action could be taken to collect on the judgment.

The two sides met in the courthouse parking lot. "You should have taken our offer," Global's lead counsel said. He smirked as he lit a cigarette. Ron was ready to punch him. Ben could see this, and quickly ended their meeting.

There was nothing left to do but try to enter the bankruptcy action in federal court and possibly collect something. The problem was that they would have to wait in line behind all of Global's creditors. The matter could go on for years with no guarantee of any recovery.

Ben decided to stay in Los Angeles to handle matters and try to sooth Ed Scott. Martha had a singles cruise planned, and left to pack. Ron made ready to go back to Arizona.

On the way out of the city he stopped to fill the tank of his rented Lincoln. The hot, smoggy air crushed him, and he was anxious to make tracks for home. As he pumped the gas, a strange man approached him.

"Senor Montgomery?" The tall, dark, elderly Hispanic gentleman looked like so many of the Mexicans living in Los Angeles. He wore a baseball cap, khaki-colored pants with sharp creases, and a dark short-sleeved shirt.

"Yeah. Do I know you?" Ron thought he'd seen him somewhere, but couldn't place him and determined he was a panhandler. Ron was not in any mood to hand over change.

"No, but I saw you in the court. I am Daniel Garcia." He was soft-spoken and direct. There was a certain gentleness about him... a softness in his eyes.

Ron vaguely recalled seeing the man in court during trial. "Well, Mr. Garcia, what is it that you want?"

"I don't want anything. I just wanted to meet you."

Ron looked at Garcia in bewilderment, then finished pumping his gas and returned the nozzle. "Yeah, well I gotta go now."

"I am a very lucky man, you know. The German Commander was very good to me." The old man then turned slowly and disappeared.

"Wait," Ron said, "what did you say?"

THE BLACK BERET

"IF THERE'S A WAY TO ATTRACT *BEAUCOUP* ATTENTION, he'll find it!"

My buddy Dennis was right. Speaking through a slight overbite and thin mustache, he recounted how Ric Vega had taken over the student union at Walden Junior College to demand a Chicano Cultural Center. This was still hot news on K-O-L-T, "The KOLT," our college radio station. We listened to the broadcast as we rode along in Jim's small Volkswagen.

Waldon is a mid-size liberal arts school, built in the 1920s, and all of its buildings covered with red tiles attesting to the popular architecture of that time.

No matter that 30 or 40 students walked in and barricaded the doors at the student union offices, it was Ric Vega who took over, then called KOLT to announce that the college board of trustees must vote to establish a cultural center for Chicano students. We always thought of these kids as "Mexican" though we knew they were born here.

I must admit that I made a claim to fame by rooming in the same place as Ric. The green, two-story house, affectionately known as The Village, outside of town was filled with students, male and female. We never knew who owned the place. Ric collected the rent from us and turned it over to a guy known only as Old Man Red. There were about 10 Waldon students there, give or take. The Village had a huge kitchen and a gigantic living room with a fireplace. A great party house.

Ric was known on campus for making noise with a bullhorn. That took guts. He wore a black beret, imagining himself as an American Che Guevara. Clearly, someone else in the family had gotten all the good looks, leaving Ric short, chubby, dark-haired with a marginal complexion. The sunken eyes and determined expression made him look tough... or so he thought. And he used that to his advantage.

"Let's go get a beer, Bill," Dennis said. We had gotten to be pretty good friends while at Walden. The two of us had been in the army in Vietnam. Dennis in artillery, and me, a motor mechanic. We met at Walden in 1971 after we got back. It was great to be home and young and living on the G.I. Bill. I still had a limp from being hit by friendly fire. Friendly fire isn't friendly, by the way. Not at all. Dennis was partially blind in one eye from a shrapnel wound.

We pulled in to Schooners, a colorful diner, where we could get a tasty burger with fries and beer for just a few bucks. While we ate, Dennis reminded me that buses would be on campus in two weeks to take students to Washington D.C. to protest the war.

"That's during finals," I said. "How can anybody go then?" It would be a total waste to go through the semester then skip out on finals.

"Well, that's when the big protest is set. Guess who's going to lead the gang?" Dennis flashed me an expressive smile.

Setting down my mug, I squinted. "You mean? No, not Vega!"

"Yes, sir. He's our man. The reincarnation of Che Guevara, complete with beret." Dennis raised two fingers, held them together and spoke. "It is written that he is the reincarnation of a homely man!"

I loved the way Dennis could sound like a guru. Feeling the beer, we laughed like crazy. Some other diners turned and gave us hard looks, but we didn't care.

"I suppose he can pick up missed courses and tests," I said. He could also pick up a few women on the trip. For some reason, Ric got lucky more than a man with his ill features had a right to. I could never understand why.

As if reading my mind, Dennis said, "He can get women, you know. Maybe not the best looking, but still..." He downed the last of his brew.

He was right. Sometimes I could hear Ric and a girl through the wood-plastered walls of The Village. I resented him and envied him at times, though his girls would never make the cover of any girly magazine.

"He probably wears the damn hat while he's in bed," I said. We paid for lunch, then returned to campus for our afternoon classes with a good buzz.

★ ★ ★

THE NIGHT BEFORE THE PROTEST IN WASHINGTON, THE phone in the kitchen rang while I sat eating a bowl of our left-over community stew. Someone had added macaroni and fresh mushrooms a few hours earlier, which was a nice touch. I picked up the receiver: it was Ric's father looking for him. After setting the receiver down, I left the kitchen and walked through the living room and past a group of kids from school watching TV. Most of them, I didn't know. I climbed the stairs and knocked on Ric's bedroom door.

"What do you want?" Ric was clearly annoyed.

"It's me... Bill. Your dad's on the phone!"

The room fell quiet, and then I heard another voice. It was Jessica Jones. Great! Now he's banging my sister's friend Jessica.

"Tell him I'll call him back!"

"Ohhhh-kay," I said. No surprise, Ric always had his way.

Back in the kitchen, I told Mr. Vega that Ric would call back. His father asked whether I could try harder to get him to the phone. I wanted to say, "Hell no, he's in bed with Jessica, the cad!" Instead, I made up an excuse that his son was visiting with an old friend. His dad accepted it.

The day ended with a late-night card game, beer, and banter about who would win the World Series.

The next morning, while Ric showered in the hallway bathroom, I saw that the door to his bedroom was open slightly. I peeked inside and saw his black beret sitting on a Styrofoam head like the ones used to display wigs at the mall. For some reason, an odd feeling overcame me. My heart began hammering.

Slowly, I stepped inside the room to get a better look. A copy of *Pedagogy of the Oppressed* by Paulo Friere sat on the dresser next to the hat. On impulse, I grabbed the hat and took off to my room. I thought I'd keep it for a while as a joke, then give it back.

I turned it over in my hands and saw that it was worn and faded. I shook my head. Is this what made him such a big shot on campus, causing fellow students to follow him, sending college administrators running for cover and drawing girls to his room?

Although I was tempted to try it on, I refused, thinking it would somehow taint my very existence. "I'll just put it back," I thought. When I walked down the dim hall, I saw Ric, in jeans and t-shirt, entering his room. I stuck the hat under my coat.

Ric turned toward me and asked, "Have you seen my hat?"

I hesitated and licked my lips. "No, why ask me?" He removed the towel from his head to reveal his nearly bald dome. I was shocked. At 23, his head was shinier than a cue ball. Funny how the mind can play tricks on you when they wear a hat all the time.

"It was right here," he said, pointing to the Styrofoam head. "I gotta get to school before the buses leave, and I can't go without it."

A sadistic wave rolled over me. It was fun to watch Ric in distress—and with such a bare head.

"Yeah, well I gotta get going, too. Hope you find it."

★ ★ ★

LATER, I SAW RIC WEARING A CRUSHED, OLD, GREEN baseball cap when a carload of students stopped by to pick him up in a dented, rusted van. I loved every minute of it.

I left for school about fifteen minutes later with the beret stuffed in my briefcase. I thought it would be really funny to give the hat to one of the winos that loitered around the pizza place across the street from the school library.

Pulling my old Chevy into the parking lot, I could see buses being loaded up. After parking, I saw Ric talking to some students. The group around him was smaller than usual. He didn't notice me. Taking a good look at Ric, he didn't seem to be radiating the usual stuff.

After grabbing some coffee at the student union, I decided I'd had enough fun and it was time to return Ric's beret. On my way to the parking lot where the buses sat, I thought Ric must be feeling like an actor in the wrong costume. Those poor dumb students needed a leader even if it was tubby Ric Vega. Though I didn't care much for him, I couldn't keep his beret, and I couldn't give it away to any stranger either.

I pulled the beret from my case. The buses were now loaded. Air brakes hissed and the diesel engines rumbled. They were about to pull away when I started jogging toward the lead bus waving the hat over my head. Again, the air brakes hissed and the bus door opened. Ric climbed out. I showed him his trademark beret.

"Where did you find this?"

"It was outside by the back door of The Village," I said.

"Well...I wonder how it got there?" Ric stared at me straight in the eye.

I cleared my throat. "I don't know. There's so many people coming over to the house... maybe somebody took it when they were drunk."

He thought a moment longer, seemed satisfied with my lie, then smiled, threw his green cap onto the trunk of a parked car, and put on his beret. The bus driver blew his horn. Ric jumped back into the bus. Students cheered and clapped. I waved and gave a thumbs up as each of the four buses passed.

Later that afternoon, while sitting in my history class, I decided to have a BBQ party at The Village on Saturday, just for the hell of it.

NIGHT LIGHT

(Based On A True Story)

THE DARK DRIVE BACK FROM SAN JOSE SEEMED QUIET AND peaceful. With Laura behind the wheel, he could rest his head and watch fence post after fence post flash by as the headlights from their small truck lit them for a moment. He was about to close his eyes when movement over flat farm fields grabbed his attention.

Something flying along shone a spotlight onto the ground.

At first, he thought it might be a crop duster, then quickly changed his mind. No, it made no sense to dust crops at night, and besides, why would it be shining a light on empty plowed fields?

Jack peered at Laura. "What is that?"

"What is what?" Laura continued looking straight ahead, her blue eyes fixed on the road.

"That thing flying over the field... with a spotlight or something going on." Jack shifted his weight and leaned back, turning to his right, and pointing his finger into the night.

Laura glanced over and adjusted her glasses. After a moment, she refocused her attention on driving. "I don't know... a low flying plane or something. Can you tell?"

She was in a hurry to get home to check on the herbs she had growing in their hot house on what they called their personal Ponderosa. Jack called it the farm, but with the ongoing dry spell, it was futile to try growing anything other than weeds. The two met at a party. They got along well, and a short time later, Jack moved in with Laura. The two-story wood farmhouse was off the beaten track in an area called Pine Glen, surrounded by trees.

"Well, it just... Wow! It just went straight up!" Jack craned his neck to look skyward. "It's gone! Did you see that?"

"No, I'm driving, Jack."

The trip to visit Jack's sister and husband had not been the most pleasant. If the two were not arguing about what to watch on TV, they fought over who left the milk out of the refrigerator.

"Well, it just looked really strange." Jack rubbed his cheeks with both hands.

"Okay we won't worry about it," Laura said.

"I can drive if you want me to." Even in the gloom of the car, Jack saw how tired Laura was. The two had lived together for seven months and had grown quite close, and he'd seen that look on her face before. She worked in admin for a temp service while he spent time maintaining his nursing studies in junior college, along with taking care of her five-bedroom house.

"Yeah, why don't you?" Laura yawned and pulled over to switch places. Jack stared into the night sky, thinking he might see the strange light again.

After about a half hour, with Laura sleeping, Jack slowed for a car stopped at the side of the dark road. Two people stood next to their car peering upward. Jack leaned forward to see what they might be looking at. An eerie glow painted the sky.

Laura woke up and stretched. She sighed and shook her head. "What's going on?"

Jack stepped out of the car without answering. A bright oval shape with orange lights circling its midsection floated through the air. It was about the size of an egg held at arm's length. At first, he thought it was silent, but then he heard a faint sound of bees buzzing. He glanced over at the other car. An elderly couple waved at him, then looked back at the lights. Their bushy white hair stood out in the night.

Laura joined him. Staring at the odd lights, a sense of calm that she had not experienced in some time washed over her. "What is that?"

Jack stared, trying to soak in the realization of what he was seeing, glad that he was not alone. "Laura, is your cell phone charged?"

Laura didn't answer. Her eyes were closed, head tilted upward, as if enjoying a refreshing breeze.

"Laura, are you okay?"

This time, Jack didn't wait for a response. He reached into the car, opened the glove compartment, and rummaged through the collection of paper, pens, and gum wrappers until he found the old phone. He turned to face the sky and raised the phone to grab a picture, but the light immediately spun and took off at an angle. It left a momentary ghostly afterglow where it had been hovering.

"Damn! I had a chance to get a picture of it!"

He turned to Laura and held her arm. She looked into his face and took a deep breath. "It was so pretty like a jewel, wasn't it, Jack?"

By this time, the older couple had returned to their car and left.

"It was almost hypnotic. I feel so relaxed." She ran fingers through her blond hair. "It was scary, though. And we're out here alone." She glanced across the landscape. "Let's go."

On the drive home, Laura grew quiet again, and dozed. Jack sensed that he did not need to tell anyone about what they had seen. Some stories are better left untold. For the rest of the trip home, no more strange lights appeared in the sky.

★ ★ ★

THE NEXT DAY, AFTER SLEEPING TILL NOON, THE TWO awoke, spent time in the shower together and had a lunch of toast, bacon, sliced apple, and coffee. Jack couldn't stop thinking about the night lights.

"That thing sure did look weird. I've never seen a flying saucer, but that's what it was, you know. A UFO from outer space." Jack stuffed his mouth.

"What thing?" Laura poured herself a second cup. "Oh, wait, you mean that dancing light? Yeah, it was pretty. But I don't know if it was from outer space." She smiled.

"Other people saw it, too, remember? I wonder if it was on the news." Jack ate the last of the heavily buttered toast. He stood, emptying his coffee cup. "I need to get to school. With some luck I can get a job as a medical technician before the end of the year."

He kissed Laura, grabbed his briefcase, then left for an afternoon class. Laura hoped that he would succeed. He was the type that started things that never got finished. The two lived well together, had enough cash, the sex was good, and as Laura thought, it was good to have a man around the house. Jack understood that the home was her place. Her place, her rules. He was never really sure how much she liked him though, and that seed of doubt had taken root.

She set out to do some house cleaning before getting her clothes together for the next day at work. She made a grocery list for Jack to take care of between classes. While walking to the road to retrieve the mail, Laura looked up and thought briefly about what she had seen the night before.

★ ★ ★

JACK CAME HOME WITH TWO OF THE BIGGEST STEAKS SHE had ever seen.

"Let's put these in the broiler," he said. After grabbing a beer from the fridge, he began looking through the cupboard for beans and vegetables to build a meal. "I had a good day at school. Learned about blood types," he laughed. "How did things go here today?"

"Fine," she said. "I wasn't able to tend to the herbs in the shed, though. I was just too tired." She paused, then grabbed his arm. "You talked to someone about the light we saw in the sky. Joe Marks was interested, but Katy Kenyon was not."

Jack faced her, his brow wrinkled. "Yeah, how do you know that?"

Laura swallowed hard and shook her head. "I don't know. It just came to me. At the market you picked up a magazine at the register then put it back. There was a cake on the cover. The lady behind you said that the frosting was such a pretty color."

"Laura, Laura, Laura. Are you following me when I leave the house?" Jack breathed deeply while tilting his head.

"No! Are you possessed?" The two had a running joke about devilish possession whenever the other acted strange.

"Laura, it's just so weird that you know that stuff about my day. I don't think I ever told you about Joe or Katy." In fact, he had not. He wondered if her apparent extrasensory perception was related to the light they saw.

"Let's just have dinner and ignore that stuff." Laura got some rolls and butter out.

Jack could not let the matter go but kept it to himself. A good dinner, some TV, Laura in bed... why ruin a good thing with talk?

★ ★ ★

THE NEXT MORNING AFTER BREAKFAST, THE TWO LEFT IN their respective vehicles for school and work. Laura walked to her desk, peppered with questions from those in the office who wanted to know about her days off and the trip to visit Jack's family. After putting on a good face about the visit, she set to shuffling paperwork.

Jack spent some time socializing before class. He chatted with other students about the anatomy lecture from the week before. Nutrition and chemistry were on the menu for this week.

Glancing across the lush campus lawn, Jack thought he saw a couple that resembled the old folks who witnessed the strange light two nights earlier. Their white hair stood out among the younger students walking about. The two were dressed in matching clothing which any other time might have been cute. But not this time.

The next thing he knew, he was standing in front of them. The couple smiled and said hello. Jack had no recollection of walking the distance from his building to where they were. He moved his mouth but no words came out. His mind went blank.

"You don't have to tell anyone about what you saw," the old man smiled. The woman grinned as she held her hand out to Jack. He took it. His words slowly returned.

"Who are you? Are you taking classes here?" Now the meeting took on a dreamlike quality. His voice sounded like he was talking through a tin can.

The woman released Jack's hand as the two turned and disappeared. Jack felt a shortness of breath. He then composed himself, as he wondered what was happening. He looked at his hand, then his watch. He'd be late for class if he didn't get a move on. Finding his seat in class, his thoughts turned to Laura and he wondered if she would know what he was doing and who he had just met.

★ ★ ★

ON HIS WAY HOME, JACK DECIDED TO STOP FOR A FAST food dinner. He bought turkey wraps and Cole slaw. When he entered the house, a can of baked beans, cornbread and beer awaited him. Jack decided to play a little game. Since he'd arrived home before Laura, he put the wraps and slaw in the fridge. As soon as Laura got home, he'd ask her what they would have for dinner. He knew she couldn't be spying on him, but the vision about Joe and Katy unnerved him.

Laura's old blue Honda pulled up to the house. The engine sound was smooth for an older sedan. Jack opened the door to greet her. It was nearly dark outside. Jack liked the fact that the old house sat on a half-acre away from any noisy or nosey neighbors. Laura stepped from the car holding what looked like a large white purse.

"Look what Laura brought home for Jack," she sang. Jack was surprised to see that the bundle she carried was a dog.

"Where did you get that?"

"It's not a *that*," Laura said. "I got him from Ana at work. She's got a litter of terriers at home and I thought that this is exactly what we need around here. Look how cute he is!"

Jack was not exactly ready to share the house with a dog, but it was Laura's place, and ultimately, she called the shots. "Well, I guess we can keep him in the bathroom till he grows up."

"We'll put him in your bed till you grow up!" she sneered.

"I didn't mean anything," Jack said, rethinking his attitude. He ruffled the dog's head. "He is cute, and he'll be a good watch dog. Does he have a name yet?"

"I thought Tubby would be a good name."

"That sounds great! Tubby. I remember how to house train puppies."

The two set about making a bed for Tubby out of a cardboard box and old blanket and towel. Laura took a can of dog food out of a bag she'd brought with her from work, and sat at the antique table in the kitchen. She looked at the refrigerator, then at Jack.

"I suppose you know what I got us for dinner," Jack said.

"I can guess... some wraps and Cole slaw maybe?"

He grabbed her arms tightly. "Laura, how did you know? How?"

"Don't get upset. It's just a guess. Let's eat."

Jack grabbed a couple of beers and opened a can of beans. As he spooned the beans into a saucepan, he paused, then turned toward Laura. "Did you gain psychic powers from seeing that light next to the road?"

"*What light?*" Laura placed the wraps on the table with cloth napkins. She loved to use them instead of paper.

Jack hesitated. "The light, Laura. *The* light." He sat and continued looking at her, waiting for a response.

"We stopped, I remember. And there was something in the sky, right? When was that?" She bit into her wrap. Tubby placed his front paws on her foot, trying to reach her knee.

"You're telling me you don't remember the UFO? The flying saucer?" Jack didn't know whether to be angry or worried.

"Don't get excited. I remember we stopped so we could switch drivers. I slept most of the way back." She sipped her beer. "A flying saucer? Really? What did it look like?"

Jack decided not to press the matter. His confusion mixed with his frustration and fear.

Dinner continued with some light conversation about Laura's work, and little Tubby. No conversation about the future. The two later climbed upstairs, showered together, made love, and went to bed with little Tubby sleeping in his own makeshift bed.

During the night, Jack awakened without warning, as if something had called him. He felt a sudden urge to go downstairs, but had no idea why. He crept down the staircase hoping not to awaken Laura. At the foot of the stairs, he glimpsed a strange glow shining on the front of the house. Peeking out a window, he saw what looked like a cloud of dust about fifty feet from the front door. At ground level, it looked about ten feet high and twice as wide. *Someone is playing a trick, a joke,* Jack thought. He could open the door to see what was going on, but not without a weapon. After grabbing a poker from the fireplace, he turned the handle slowly, eased the door open, and peeked out.

Adrenaline raced through his body. He inhaled deeply and said, "You better get outta here! I'll call my dog on you!" Jack grinned to himself, thinking of little Tubby chasing drunken teenagers down the dirt road. "I mean it!"

Suddenly, Jack felt empty, as if all thought and emotion were drained from him. A voice in his head said that he didn't need *that,* and he knew immediately *that* referred to the poker. Then he thought... *a glowing cloud cannot hurt me.* As he stepped out and walked toward the light, he thought he saw a shadowy figure. Even though he was not afraid, he closed his eyes briefly.

When he blinked, Jack was upstairs in the bedroom again, staring out the window. A dark human figure, suspended in air, floated away from the window until it completely disappeared.

★ ★ ★

THE NEXT MORNING, JACK AWAKENED WITH A SEARING headache. Laura gave him some aspirin and made breakfast. She put Tubby in the laundry room which doubled as a pantry and storage for tools, some coats, and shoes. He would have to stay there until Jack got home. His new job would be house training the dog. Laura left for work.

Moments later, Jack headed for the door. He glanced toward the fireplace and noticed the poker was gone. Then he remembered. He'd gone outside the night before... There was a strange, glowing cloud... *The figure in the window!*

Did that really happen? Was it a dream?

Trembling, Jack shuffled to the porch and sat in one of the old rockers. He gazed past the wood columns of the old house where the cloud had been. The day was beautiful. A breeze whispered among the trees, and the clear, blue sky gave Jack a good feeling. He decided not to worry about what happened. He'd heard about so-called *lucid* dreams, but this was not the same. Another phenomenon a friend told him about was that a person might confuse a dream event with something that actually happened. The possible causes confused him.

After dressing and gathering his books, Jack left for school wondering if his vision from last night was just a bad dream. If that was all there was, he could have convinced himself. But there was Laura's strange clairvoyance thing, and the old couple, too...

Every now and then, during his classes, Jack thought about the night before. The day was consumed by lectures on chemistry, nursing practice and theory, and psychology. Despite the volume of information thrown at him, he could not stop thinking about his dream.

Late in the day, with no relief from his apparent vision, he took his course books to the library. After obtaining an internet access card, he searched for *dreams*, and *memory*, and finally *UFOs*. Some of the most interesting stories came up under the last category.

Jack began reading. He came across one story that caught his attention. In Texas one night, in 1980, two women and a seven-year-old—a grandson of one of the ladies—encountered a diamond shaped UFO shooting flames from its underside onto the road in front of them. They stopped their car to observe. The craft blocked their path. They all got out of the car, shielding their faces from the flaming downspout. Frightened, one woman took the boy back to the car, but the other lady became fascinated with the sight. The heat finally drove her back to the car where she turned on the air conditioner. Within a few minutes, a dozen helicopters converged on the area. They attempted to encircle the other craft, which one of the women later described as a *flaming diamond.*

Jack gulped. Chills raced over his shoulders, neck, and cheeks.

Investigators were only able to conclude that the witnesses had encountered a craft of undetermined origin.

Another internet search disclosed an incident involving an Army Reserve helicopter and a bright green light during a 1983 night-flight in Ohio. At around 11:00 p.m. en route from Columbus to Cleveland, one of the four crew members saw the light off to the side of the helicopter on an apparent collision course with an estimated airspeed of 500 knots. The pilot initiated a controlled free fall dive to avoid impact.

The crew estimated the UFO to be about 60 feet in length, with a red light at one end and a green light beam at the other. It was a gray metallic color with some green light reflecting off the craft. Despite the controlled free fall, the helicopter gained 400 feet in altitude. The interior of the chopper turned green as the alien craft shone its light inside before suddenly disappearing.

The four crew members issued a signed report on the incident. The strange object was also observed by witnesses on the ground. The magnetic compass in the helicopter never worked properly after the incident and was eventually replaced.

The military officially concluded that the crew had seen another aircraft that was in the area.

Trying not to let the stories disturb him, Jack drove home thinking he would feel better after seeing Laura again. Inside the house, Jack found Tubby in the pantry. The room smelled of urine. He escorted the puppy outside to see what he had left in him, and to wait for Laura to return from work. Darkness settled in as Tubby wandered off.

Jack continued mulling over the UFO stories when, without warning, he heard the sound of crunching dry leaves. He turned and almost lost his balance. The white-haired old man—the same one from campus and from the road trip home—walked toward him. Jack licked his lips and apprehensively stepped back, but to his surprise, he suddenly felt at ease. The old man smiled and handed the fireplace poker to Jack.

"May we speak inside for a moment? Alone?" the man asked. Jack agreed, and the two strode toward the house. He was astonished at how easily he agreed to invite this stranger inside without question.

When they reached the porch, the headlights from Laura's car flooded the scene. Jack, poker in hand, stood ready to introduce the old man, not knowing who he was. He turned to face the headlights. In an odd way, her car lights reminded him of what he had seen in the night sky just two days ago.

Laura stepped out. She carried a large bag over her shoulder. She surveyed the yard. "Hey Jack, where's Tubby? He's not still in the pantry, is he?"

Jack turned to introduce the old man. He was gone. He spun all the way around, desperately looking for him.

"What are you doing, Jack? Is that a welcome home dance?" Laura's voice, ringing with sarcasm, lowered as she climbed the stairs to the front door.

Jack, shaken and pale with fright, leaped up the steps, bursting through the doorway past Laura. "Did you see where the old man went? He was standing next to me."

"What old man?" She furrowed her brow. "You look like you saw a ghost. You're scaring me!" After setting her bag down, Laura held Jack's shoulders to confirm he was not playing a joke. "What are you doing with the poker?" The two went inside.

"The old man gave it back to me. He was there, then he was gone." Jack crept to the window next to the door, and peeked outside.

"What are you talking about? Where's Tubby?" Laura yelled.

"I'm not going outside without a light" said Jack, his voice nearly trembling. "Tubby ran outside."

Laura, tears welling in her eyes, grabbed a flashlight. Jack carefully stepped out, his head on a swivel.

"We have to be careful. That strange old man is out here." Jack wiped a bead of sweat from his forehead. "If we put some dog food on the porch, Tubby will come back."

Laura ignored him. She stepped farther into some weeds and brush, calling Tubby. Jack told her not to step out too far. He stayed near the house while Laura searched slowly into the night. She thought she heard a bark at one point. Racing toward the sound, she tripped and screamed. Jack bit his lip, then ran to help her.

Jack found her quickly and helped her back inside the house. Laura wept as Jack scooped some dog food into Tubby's dish and placed it outside the front door. He pulled some cans of stew out for dinner, but Laura told him to eat it himself as she hobbled upstairs. Jack tried to follow her up but she told him to sleep downstairs and let Tubby in if he comes back.

After trying to eat some stew, Jack sank into one of the stuffed chairs. He felt more alone than ever. He wondered if he was, in fact, losing his mind. He got up and turned on all the lights downstairs, then checked the lock on every door and window. He finally settled down after kicking off his shoes and stretching out on the sofa. A heavy red throw completed his bed for the night. He finally fell asleep thinking about how angry Laura was and how she might be thinking he was on drugs. Maybe he was being irrational.

At about three in the morning, a rumble shook the house. Jack jumped up at the sound of something scraping on the front door. Then he heard Tubby yelping. At the same time, spotlights flashed past the windows. Jack ran to the door, opening it as Tubby ran inside, his hair dirty and wet. Tree branches waved back and forth against the sky, as if from the wash of helicopter blades. Jack slammed the door. What would a helicopter be doing here shining a light?

Jack grabbed a dish towel from the kitchen, then chased after Tubby up the stairs to where Laura slept. Jack wrapped Toby in the towel, then opened the bedroom door. Laura sat up. Jack sat on the bed holding Tubby. Laura grabbed the dog and held him, crying all the while.

"Where was he?" she asked, wiping her nose on a robe she wore to bed.

"He came to the front door," Jack said, still catching his breath.

"Thank God. I thought he was gone for good, eaten by a coyote or something."

A few silent moments passed.

"Did you hear the helicopter?" Jack said.

"I didn't hear anything until you opened *my door.*"

From Laura's tone, Jack decided the best course would be to say goodnight and go downstairs. "Okay, well he's home now, so nothing to worry about." Jack turned to go, waiting for Laura to say something more.

"Make sure all the doors are locked, Jack. See you in the morning." Laura held Tubby in her pink robe.

Jack grabbed a pillow and returned to his makeshift bed, hoping he had not damaged their relationship beyond repair.

Eventually, sleep overcame him. He dreamed of driving in a strange area when he saw two creepy looking boys about three feet tall near the middle of the road. They wore what looked like school uniforms. Wide striped blazers with two rows of shiny buttons, along with a short black visor fronting a skull cap. Their pants were gray and baggy. The two each wore large round-lens glasses, and their faces were expressionless.

Jack felt the hair on the back of his neck stand up as he stepped on the gas to get past the two, but the car's engine shuddered, then stalled. He tried turning the ignition but that only made the steering wheel bend. Suddenly, one of them appeared at the driver's side window while the other leaned over the hood in front of the windshield. The two were now larger, at least six feet tall. Jack tried to cry out but could only stare into the pale faces of the two...

★ ★ ★

JACK AWAKENED AS THE SUN ROSE, STILL TERRORIZED BY what he had seen in his dream, and confused about his surroundings. He lay on the ground inside the shed where

Laura grew herbs. He sat up, wondering *what in hell am I doing here?*

Tubby ran out the front door barking at the shed. Laura followed. Looking inside, she saw Jack brushing dirt off himself. "What are you doing in here?"

"I don't know," he said. "I don't know how I got here! I went to sleep in the living room and woke up here!"

Laura's face stiffened and she crossed her arms across her chest. "Give up whatever you and your school buddies are taking Jack. I mean it!"

"We're not taking anything. All this weird stuff started the night we saw that big light in the sky. You say you don't remember it."

"I don't remember because *it didn't happen.*"

"Don't say that," he growled. "You got out of my truck and looked straight at it, Laura." Jack's anger made her step back. Then she noticed that most of the small herb plants were missing. There were empty spaces now where four-inch clay pots had been.

"What happened to the basil, dill, and coriander, Jack? Did you hide them in your sleep, too?" Her voice rang in a low tone of anger.

"I don't know. I don't know anything!" Jack stepped out from the shed toward the house. On the way, he stopped, wide-eyed, nearly covering his mouth. He whispered to himself, "Oh shit! *They* told me to give them the plants."

Laura rushed past him, carrying Tubby. She was not going to tell Jack to leave. Not yet. He might become angry, or even violent. The best thing to do was go to work, take Tubby, and talk to Jack afterward. With Jack so irrational, who knows what he might do? She might even have to call the law to get him out of the house. She left without breakfast, telling

Jack that he should see a doctor. He listened while nodding his head.

Jack spent the day wandering about the house. Then, he stepped out to the shed. He vaguely recalled hearing a voice in his head telling him that the herbs looked very good, and that they were needed for study. Jack allowed them to be taken away.

Then he remembered the dream.

Two weird looking boys who grew taller.

He was not afraid now. It was just a dream.

He returned to the house, showered, then stretched out in bed feeling very relaxed. He awoke to the sound of Laura's voice. "Wake up Jack. Did you go to school today?"

"What?" Jack raised his head, feeling intoxicated. "I'm so tired, what time is it?"

"It's time for you to wake up and get something to eat. Put on some clothes and come downstairs. I got a pizza."

Jack made his way down, barefoot, in a t-shirt and faded jeans. Laura made coffee to bring Jack to full awareness.

"Did you make an appointment to see a doctor?" As far as Laura was concerned, this was a test for Jack. She would not be living with a scatterbrain who talked of invisible people in the yard and slept outside.

"No, I just got so sleepy. I can do that tomorrow." He took a huge bite of pizza, then licked his fingers. He gulped lukewarm coffee as if he was a man lost in the desert, swallowing water.

That was it. Laura would have to get him out. He seemed like such a good guy when they met. He had a future. He seemed dependable. Now he was just a strange man confused by a light he said he saw in the sky.

After their dinner, Jack said he was going upstairs to sleep. Laura objected, telling him she would make a bed for him downstairs. He brushed her off while climbing the stairs.

Laura, disgusted, stayed up late writing down everything that happened since the drive home from San Jose. She would need it later to demonstrate Jack's behavior and the deterioration of what she thought was a promising relationship. She later went up to bed, placing Tubby in between her and Jack.

After about four hours, Laura woke up to find Jack standing at the window spreading the lace curtains.

"Jack, what are you doing?" Fearful, Laura prepared to run to the door.

"It's back," he said. "Come and see." Jack's voice was so calm, so peaceful, so inviting.

Laura saw some light streaming in the window and decided, against her better judgment, to go ahead and look. She picked up Tubby and stepped to the window.

There it was.

A round pulsing light, white on top, turning orange underneath. It began moving slowly side to side.

"Oh my God! What is it?" Laura could hardly breathe.

Jack held her, telling her he remembered now that he was told there was nothing to be afraid of.

"Laura, I need to see it closer. I need to get close to it."

"Jack, don't go. We don't know what that is. Stay here!"

"Don't worry, I'll be back. Wait for me."

He hugged Laura and Tubby and, still in his underwear, left the room. Laura curled up in bed wondering what to do. Should she call the local sheriff? How would she explain this? She decided to call. The last thing she remembered was reaching for the phone, then standing at the window mesmerized by the light, feeling unbridled serenity, and wishing the light would take her away.

The sheriff's dispatcher, thinking she had received a crank call, didn't send anyone out to the house until the next morning. A deputy found every door and window in the house wide open.

★ ★ ★

JACK AND LAURA WERE NEVER SEEN AGAIN. SOME SAY they were kidnapped, or had been murdered and buried. Little Tubby was found sitting on the front porch, a strange oval shaped tattoo inside his ear.

If only he could talk.

MATING RITUAL

My folks told me, "Listen to us, Katie O'Tool. You must not marry that guy Eddie!"

I was way too young to know better. And I always loved the rumble of a Harley—there is nothing else like it. So, my folks didn't stand a chance of changing my mind.

We were heading north for some R&R. The thundering sound of Eddie's Harley Davidson was music to my ears and there was no better time to escape. Summer heat brought the urge to breathe cool country air. In an hour, me and Eddie would meet up with the others.

His bike was custom built with a fully extended front fork—the first in town. Ed and Danny, nicknamed "Handsome," built the bike in Handsome's monster garage while listening to Led Zeppelin blasting on an eight-track.

The sparkling lime-green bike with gold trim and knucklehead engine was pieced together from old parts... some stolen, and some provided by outlaw bikers who were sometimes paid with weed and booze. That beautiful machine made Eddie feel tall, bigger than Handsome's six-foot frame.

Eddie was a Latin kid with super long black hair, who wore thick scars on his knuckles.

Women hang with the club for the biker life. They're not chained to it. The guys knew women would come to them and expect to be told how to behave. I felt at the time that I was at a point where I could overlook most of Eddie's hurtful transgressions. Their behavior was part of the culture, and I accepted it even though I didn't really like it.

But I loved those rides. When I mounted up behind Eddie, life couldn't get any better. I imagined how great I looked, too, in aviator glasses, a long-sleeved denim shirt, my curly blond hair flowing like a windy wave.

★ ★ ★

I GOT TO KNOW EDDIE WHILE WE WERE IN JUNIOR HIGH. Both our families went to a Catholic church, and each Sunday we exchanged glances until we were sitting together. One Sunday, I wrote down my phone number and school name— Valley View—then gave it to Eddie.

Eddie lived in the south end of town where he went to Richmond School. Yard fights there took place daily, with an occasional knifing after school just for kicks. The place was an even mix of black, white, and Latin kids.

I was just 15 when I left Valley during lunch time and walked with a girlfriend to visit Eddie at Richmond. We found a secluded spot behind a classroom to make out. We kept our love secret from our parents, and each day our love grew. Once, he wanted to find a place to make out at church. I told him we would not do anything like that. We wanted to be married, but Eddie said no one would allow us unless I was pregnant.

Eddie's family lived on a main commercial street in a house sandwiched between a mechanic shop and a liquor store. His mom and dad were a bad combination. His old man never failed to find reasons to disparage Eddie, his brother and sister. His mom sent dad to jail for abuse when Eddie was 12. From that time on, Eddie lived in anger.

As a kid, he met bikers hanging out at the mechanic's shop. He asked about their bikes and the vests they wore, called "colors." They talked with the "little guy," offered him smokes and beer on occasion. When the guys fired up their bikes, Eddie dreamed of going with them.

★ ★ ★

AS OUR FOUR BIKES ROUNDED A CURVE, I THOUGHT OF US as a squadron of fighter airplanes. A rusted white '59 Ford station wagon followed us like a heavy bomber. Frank and Annie drove that. They were students at Saylor Jr. College and loved to travel with the club. They loved being a small part of it. Bob "The Blob," a friend of Annie's, granted their request to hang out with us.

During that ride, I spread my arms wide, imagining the thrill of flight, and loving the time away from my two-year-old daughter. Soon enough, we caught up with the others. After a while, our caravan went off road to a secluded shady spot.

★ ★ ★

IN OUR FIRST YEAR OF HIGH SCHOOL, EDDIE FINALLY convinced me that I should become pregnant so that we could marry. With a plan, help from friends, and a borrowed Pontiac

GTO, we set off for the drive in. Eddie wanted to smoke some marijuana before we started. I told him, "No," and that our baby would be born retarded if we did that. Half undressed, we started. In a short time, we finished, awkwardly, in the back seat while Sean Connery led his team of scuba divers in a fight during a scene from *Thunderball.*

My parents knew nothing about Eddie. As time went on, the two of us met at a friend's place, or in a car. I always thought that what we were doing was right. It took some time but soon I was pregnant with Eddie's baby. Not long after, I broke the news to my parents. Me and Eddie were married at the courthouse. Mom and Dad were so disappointed that we weren't married in church, but I couldn't do that.

★ ★ ★

OUR BIKES FOLLOWED A NARROW DUSTY TRAIL. Everyone stopped at the end where a stone cabin sat, nearly camouflaged entirely by brush. A nearby sign, marked with bullet holes, read, " *Welcome* ". This was our club retreat.

We rolled to a stop and the next thing was to dismount. I called for help as I struggled to get my short legs in gear. Eddie had already hopped off and, ignoring me, walked on to meet up with the others, so I swung my leg over and slid off the seat. I noticed that Jeff, aka "Boxer" helped his woman, Clara. She was nursing a broken nose and was careful not to get blood or snot on Boxer's colors. Bob The Blob straightened up, challenging himself to a spitting contest from his bike. Mary, his "date" hopped off.

Handsome and Blaster stepped to the cabin door. Before they could knock, Old Man Gavin opened up. He was so happy to see them. They hugged each other like long lost brothers. The Blob handed Gavin some cash and a bag of weed.

The teen tagalongs, Frank and Annie, unloaded their canvas and wood folding chairs with a large ice chest, as if we were at a school picnic. This was a cheap outing for them. They liked the shiny bikes and the excitement of watching the ride. They didn't have a clue about how this one would end.

Gavin stepped forward to greet everyone. He eyeballed the shiny bikes. "Well, the gang's all here!"

I remember his long gray hair blowing in the breeze. He said hello to Clara and me. I tried to smile at what looked like a skinny, yellow-eyed fiend from a horror movie.

He asked Eddie, "Whatever happened to that guy with the bike that had a chrome oversized gas tank?"

"Oh, we used to call him The Crank. Yeah, old Cranky from San Bernardino," Eddie said. "Well, he had a run in with the cops. Got his ass arrested for possession of drugs after a chase. While he was on probation, he took off by himself to Big Bear. Nobody has seen him since."

Laughing, Gavin told Eddie to go inside and bring out some beer. Eddie, with Boxer's help, brought out some quart bottles.

Gavin told us we were free to build a campfire. He said he had something for us. He disappeared inside the cabin for a few minutes and returned with a bottle of Southern Comfort and a hash pipe. He said these "goodies" were great companions for campfire stories. I frowned at the thought that sometimes stories turned from laughter, to conflict, to punches. I worried about my Eddie.

I wondered when and how I accepted all this as normal... whatever normal was.

As shadows set in, the guys cleaned up an old fire ring. We found some ancient wood benches and stumps to sit on.

Handsome watched Annie pull a small camera from the wagon. "Be sure and get my good side, Annie," he said. I could tell that Annie was out of sorts because of the scars on Handsome's face. He called them *badges* from a fight while a soldier at Fort Benning. A giant brawl erupted over someone's bad words, and Handsome jumped into a fight between blacks, Puerto Ricans, and rednecks. He forgot long ago which side he was on. Later, he called the melee *beautiful.*

Everyone gathered around the fire drinking and smoking. Amid the laughter and stories, someone yelled, "I'm gettin' hungry." I went to Eddy's bike for some jerky from a saddle bag. We had more than enough for the bunch. It was home made by my mom from London Broil, spicy, and nearly an inch thick.

Eddie began telling a story about how, as a kid, he watched some guys build a bike in one afternoon from parts. The guys started with a panhead frame. An engine got delivered on the back of a pickup. With wiring, wheels, gas tank, and other parts, the bike was completed in about 6 hours. He said it was a testament to how much these builders knew their stuff. Real craftsmen.

Staring into the fire, after drinking more than enough Southern Comfort and not listening to Eddie, I reflected on the time I found out about some girl Eddie knocked up. He took her to a concert less than a year after we were married. I figured this was the only one that I *knew about.* Another girl Eddie messed with had an abortion. Her family disowned her after that. When I confronted Eddie, he grabbed me by the neck, squeezed hard, and told me to forget about it. He knew how to keep me quiet.

Sometimes the guys would bring Eddie home after heavy drinking. It was not unusual for me to find him at the door, drunk and bleeding, then telling me how a bunch of the guys kicked ass. As I got to know him better, I learned to see him as a loving father, but also an abuser, a womanizing cad. He would grow out of it, I thought. *He'll grow up.*

I drank again from the bottle as it was passed to me.

Someone gave me the hash pipe and I passed it on. Some of the others laughed at me. "Does she have to be at work in the morning?" One of the women teased, "Are you pregnant, Katie?" More laughter. I began to think of my daughter, Mia, who just turned two. My folks always took good care of her.

A full moon showed itself from behind some scattered clouds.

Handsome gazed up. "Man, look at that," he said. A few minutes later, he added, "Wolves should be painted on the bike's gas tanks." He then told the story of how he outran a cop near Palm Springs by going off road. Handsome was like that, a poet or an artist one minute, and a law-flouting rebel the next.

Between the beer and smoke, Eddie interrupted the conversation, bragging about being the first in town to have extended front forks on his bike.

This proved too much for Handsome. He jumped in and, in an amused voice, said, "I bet you thought you were hot shit, eh Eddie?"

Eddie threw Handsome a hard look. He stood up, angry as his father would be. Handsome pretended to reach for the buck knife on his waist. Eddie, fuming, stepped toward Handsome.

I got up and stumbled toward Eddie. I squeezed his bicep from behind trying to stop a potential slug out from igniting.

The only time I had ever grabbed him like that was soon after our marriage, when I tried to stop him from leaving the house to meet a girl he knew. At the time, he yanked himself away and left on his bike.

Eddie froze. He turned, grabbing me by each arm and backed me up to the station wagon. He started slapping me. Hard. Left... Right... Left... He kept smashing my face harder and harder.

"Hey! This is a party, not a fight!" Handsome yelled.

Eddie had bloodied his hand. Boxer moved in and shouted, "Leave it alone, Eddie!"

I slumped against the wagon and cried for help. Clara brought over a sweater. She wrapped it over my shoulders. Eddie lowered his fists, then turned away and faced the others.

I couldn't stand it anymore. I was so damn mad! Bending down, mopping rosy phlegm from my face, I picked up a flat rock. I swung it at the side of Eddie's head. He slumped to his knees, then fell on his stomach. I threw the rock at him, hitting him on his back.

"Oh, shit!" Blaster jumped up and grabbed me. Eddie lay motionless on the ground with blood seeping from his scalp and ears.

Blaster kneeled at Eddie's side. "Hey man, can you hear me?"

There was no response.

He checked his breathing and pulled his eyelids up with his grimy fingers. "Man, he's out for the count." Blaster flashed back to Vietnam. He said once that the stupidest thing he ever did was go airborne. And he wouldn't talk about his service any more than that.

"He's breathing, but he needs medical." He stood, wiping blood on his pants. The others had gathered around at this point, and several of them eyed me with pure evil on their faces.

Clara pulled me aside. "Honey, what have you done? Man, you don't want to be around when he wakes up."

"If he *does* wake up," Annie whispered to Frank.

The guys decided to take Eddie somewhere for help. "Wow, how exciting!" Annie said to Frank.

After a huddle, they decided that Blaster would take me home on his bike. I agreed, and wept, holding a dirty hankie to my face. All I wanted was to be home.

Frank tugged on Annie's sleeve. "What if this guy dies?"

"Get a grip and man up, Frank," Annie said.

Gavin brought out some blankets. He helped the others roll Eddie up like a carpet. There was a Ranger Station down the road that could offer help. Eddie was carefully placed in the back of the wagon.

"The party's over, but the drama was worth it. Too bad about Eddie. He's tough. He'll be okay," Gavin said, his eyes glazed over. "Katie, I don't know how you're gonna get right with Eddie on this one. I'll take care of Eddie's bike, don't worry about that."

As everyone packed up, I joined Blaster. He helped me onto his bike and I wrapped my arms around his waist. I breathed deeply as we set off. An hour later, we pulled into my driveway. Dazed from booze and the ride, we got off the bike and stretched. I remember running to a side door, saying, "I have to pee!"

Blaster pushed the bike into my single car, wood frame garage. He stepped into the small house, hoping to get some sleep. I doctored my face with cold water in the bathroom, then returned with a warm washcloth. I handed it to Blaster. He rubbed his face and neck, then under his arms.

I looked at the couch, then toward the bedroom. I had to think about what I really wanted. I was not the sixteen-year-old looking forward to what I thought would be love and a family with Eddie. I remembered the fun times as kids: sneaking around, having our fun with friends. I was happy during the first part of my marriage.

But not now.

At first, I felt bad about stoning Eddie. I wasn't brought up that way. At the same time, it felt like an end to one life, and the start of a new one. It was scary.

Then I wondered, what would Mia be like, as she grew up, if I stayed with Eddie?

I gazed down at the carpet, then looked up at Blaster. He wore a sheepish look on his face. I smiled and said, "You can sleep in the bed, if you like."

"You mean in the bed or on it?"

"Get in. I'll be right back."

I entered the bedroom wearing my lacy black underwear. Blaster sat, bare chested, on the edge of the bed. "Are you sure about this?" he said.

I slowly removed my bra. "I am sure..."

He leaned back and kicked off his boots. Then he stood up and nearly lost his balance removing his jeans. I eased him onto his back and straddled him. Brushing his hair, I asked, "What's your real name anyway?"

He hesitated. "Cornelius. My name is Cornelius. It's from the Latin. The sisters at church told me it means 'horn'."

Laughing, I kissed him and closed my eyes. I let go and felt truly free.

★ ★ ★

We woke up at 2 o'clock in the afternoon. Agonizing pain in my face kept me from looking in the mirror. I said, "Oh God, look what time it is. I have to see about Eddie!"

Blaster eased out of bed. "You'll have to stay away from each other, you know. Maybe for all time." He pulled on his pants.

I had to face reality. I threw on some clothes. Eddie would never forgive me; I knew that much.

"Kate, he never really loved you. You know that, eh?"

"*It was a sick love.*" I wept and covered my face. Blaster moved in to hug me. I stepped back. "You need to leave. I'll call my sister to come over with my kid."

Blaster nodded and turned away.

"Wait a sec," I said, and held his hand.

He stopped and faced me.

"Thank you for everything, Blaster."

He cleared his throat and whispered, "I'd prefer it if you called me Cornelius. Would that be okay?"

I smiled and squeezed his hand.

★ ★ ★

Me and Eddie finally split. He got the bike, tools, record player and TV. Child visitation times were never set by the court. I was barely able to pay rent and feed my daughter, so I took a job sorting books at the local library. I'm living a much simpler existence now. My life goes on with a strange feeling of joy and fright at the sound of a Harley engine on the street. And I often wonder where Blaster ended up.

I heard later that Frank and Annie got married. At their ceremony, he wore a full beard, and Annie had more tattoos and silver piercings than a New Orleans hooker. They rode off on a 1976 V-Twin Superglide Liberty. I think of them sometimes while sorting books.

THE LAWYER CUP

FERRIS WEIL AWAKENS TO CLASSICAL MUSIC. JUDGE IGOR Dresden loves putting on the sound of what he calls motivation incarnate. The two share a beautiful old two-story wood frame home surrounded by a lovely orange grove. The house, far enough from town to avoid traffic and noise, is still close enough to walk or jog to the small-town center where one can shop or have coffee. The judge had allowed Ferris to stay in the home rather than live under foster care.

Ferris, almost 17 now, still feeling the effects of what the two drank the night before, begins his recall of what the judge had said. Ferris is special; a beautiful future awaits him; the judge is someone Ferris can look up to, thus he is allowed the honor of drinking from the Lawyer Cup. Its resemblance to a silver chalice is unmistakable. The judge, while explaining to Ferris the meaning of his importance in the world, took young Ferris into the study, where after some banter, the two performed some role play.

While getting out of bed, Ferris wonders *did we shower together again last night?*

Ferris, one of four boys, found trouble whenever he left his mother's house. She gave up on him after his repeated violations of the law. She wanted him placed in a group home. He would fight with other kids just because he could. His height and heavy hands made him the winner many times over, and he would celebrate by kicking in a car window to hear the alarm. When other kids heard an alarm they yelled, *Ferris strikes again!*

On the street, Ferris would angle for a ride in a patrol car. He loved wrestling with police when he was found. He believed the conflict made him the tough guy in everyone's mind. The day Ferris drew blood was the day he sliced a kid who called Ferris a stupid ass. The name caller, bigger than Ferris, survived. Just a few stitches on the cheek and ear. Ferris then got his first taste of confinement in "juvie" lockdown.

★ ★ ★

DRESDEN, A STOCKY MAN, COVERING HIS CURLY HEAD with a golf cap, gets into his sporty Mustang convertible, leaving Ferris to his video games and graphic novels. The activity would keep him occupied until Dresden returned home. The judge's goal is always to keep Ferris happy so that he would never think of leaving.

Arriving at the courthouse, Dresden greets his staff and prepares to deal with the morning docket. He spent the previous day reading memos, reports and declarations relating to County Child Support Services, Juvenile Hall incarcerations or releases, and other related family law matters. During these sessions, many youth offenders appear with their representatives. The judge occasionally allows the minors to speak to their plight. He enjoys the power. He loves telling his court clerk, Cayenne Hopper, a slim redhead, that if not for the guidance received from above in making decisions, that the youth who appear before him would be left to a thoroughly misguided life... left to fend for themselves on the streets, prey to criminal elements, spending wasted lives in jail, or worse, preying on others.

Cayenne, helpful in every way, operates by the book: Judge Dresden the master, and she the loyal servant. Her skill is instrumental in getting the paperwork done, with court administration help, to have Ferris declared a ward of the state and thereby move into Dresden's home, as he requested. A short news story about the matter announces the court's willingness to take on the burden and share in the reshaping of a young life.

When Cayenne's husband is away on his job hauling lumber interstate, she spends time with Judge Dupont Elder. She thinks of the relationship as a beautiful secret. In reality, it is as secret as a movie poster for a vulgar drama.

Old Man Elder, as he is called by his staff and the bar, sports silver-gray hair, somewhat curly, with a beard reaching from ear to ear. The absence of a moustache makes him appear to be one of the pioneers who settled the county. His gambling habit keeps him perpetually poor, yet he is always able to put on a great party for members of the legal community. His wife, finally ending their stagnant relationship, enjoys her new life with a successful personal injury lawyer.

As Dresden enters his courtroom, his bailiff calls the court to order. All rise until told to be seated. Dresden gives his usual greeting, and a few eager responses follow in return. The numerous files piled high on the bench only delight the judge.

The court reporter, Hellzel, considers her job a grim duty. She is rude and self-centered, and her good looks fool many a male lawyer into thinking a luncheon date might be in the offing. Hellzel loves only cats. On her walk to the parking lot after work, she makes it a point to tell panhandlers to shut up as she hurries to her shiny new Jaguar.

The court bailiff, Deputy Trout, in his tan uniform, stands near the door leading to Dresden's chambers like a sentry. His waistline is trim from visits to the gym each day, and he is already thinking about lunch with the court staff—a lunch usually paid for by Dresden. Trout is also thinking about interesting property confiscated and located in the evidence lockers at headquarters. He would be looking over some of the items in the late afternoon for the first pick.

Dresden calls the first case: The Matter of Ariel Passover. Two people step up to the counsel table. The expression on young Ariel's plump face never changes while standing before the court. The family had designated Dewey Cheetum as her Next Friend to handle the minor's case. The Judge hears that local stores can't leave any goods near the front entrance without Ariel putting them in her bag and hurrying off. Dewey explains that Ariel merely needs understanding, not punishment. The trashy mobile home park where she lives is about to be closed down. The family is in disarray.

Dresden sees Ariel as a needy girl who could benefit from a short stay in Juvenile Hall for her misdeeds. She might even lose weight during vigorous morning exercise, he thinks. He gives an order to send Ariel to Juvenile Hall until a suitable foster home is designated. Someone would find and care for her just as Dresden cares for Ferris.

Though the docket is larger than usual, the court day ends in time for Trout to zip on over to the department evidence room. Cayenne takes her special folder to the court's law library where she privately figures how much cash she can remove from traffic fine money held by admin to add to her new clothes and shoes fund. The process was figured out long ago, by her book.

Dresden stops at a local deli after work for gourmet sandwiches and wine. A nice dinner with Ferris would include Chardonnay with a small treatment. On arrival home, Dresden finds the front door unlocked. He enters, calling Ferris. A search throughout the house leaves Dresden more than anxious. The boy had taken his things: comics, games, everything purchased by Dresden. And the Cup. The Cup is missing! He seeks to contain his nerves by opening the wine. How could Ferris leave after all the love he gave him?

* * *

ALMOST TWO YEARS LATER, THE ARBITRATION AGREED to by the parties, is nearly finalized. This procedure avoids a court trial and will resolve matters quickly. Ferris, now an adult, tells his story of alleged abuse by Judge Dresden. He recounts drinking from the Lawyer Cup, the shared showers, scars on his body, and the drugging and mental distress.

Dresden hires his friend Phelony Lynn to put on his defense during the action brought by Ferris. In business for over 20 years, Phelony has her own problems: bringing meritless actions, commingling client funds, failure to represent clients competently. Little things as she puts it. She complains of state bar bias and their unfair costs and fees.

During the course of investigation, Dresden's home computer is taken for inspection. He is asked previously, under oath, whether it had been tampered with. "No," he says. Today, the Arbitrator, a retired judge, hopes to complete matters and render a decision.

Ferris sits inside the meeting room with a pretty, young brown-haired girl by his side holding his hand. Dresden enters with Lynn. They sit at the conference table. The Arbitrator reminds the group that Dresden and Ferris are still under oath.

Judge Dresden is asked again whether he had tampered with the home computer. Again, he said, "No."

"Are you certain?" the Arbitrator persists.

Dresden forcefully states that he was sure. The Arbitrator then opens a file which, with the help of State Judicial Commission investigators, reveals that the computer hard drive had indeed been tampered with at certain times. Voice and video of Dresden and Ferris together was located and removed by state investigators onto a separate disk.

The Arbitrator hands the file to Ms. Lynn. She reads and shows it to Dresden. He glances at it, looks toward Ferris, then hands it to the Arbitrator. Phelony and Dresden ask if they could speak outside in the hall.

Within 10 days a settlement is reached. Ferris is awarded $300,000. His lawyer takes 30%. With what Ferris and his girlfriend, Vicky, are able to keep, the two could move out of state. He plans to open a custom car body and paint shop. Vicky wants to learn to be a hairdresser. Life never looked so dazzling. A fresh start.

Ferris and Vicky move away to Nevada. They rent a small apartment and begin enjoying their new life and all the dreams they have.

At first, times are good. Living in a big, beautiful apartment complex with a pool on the edge of Las Vegas makes them feel like some kind of celebrities. Vicky opens a cosmetologist school. Ferris finds a job at a mechanic shop, fueling delivery trucks and checking tire pressures.

Shortly thereafter, Vicky develops a natural curiosity about gambling, and hits the casinos with girls from the school quite often after classes. It doesn't take long for her to lose the award money. Heavy drinking follows. Some days, she misses school completely.

Ferris feels that tasks he is given at work are beneath him. He gets into arguments with the guys in the shop. One day, he takes a swing at a supervisor which promptly gets him fired.

After losing his job, he meets a drug dealer living in the apartment complex. He gives up an honest living to work with the dealer. Ferris soon becomes addicted to the product.

After six months of partying with strangers, most of the money is gone along with their counterfeit friends. Payments on the new car are overdue, as well as rent. Worse, the partnership with the dealer has gone bad. He sends messengers daily to collect. Ferris and Vicky decide to gather what few possessions they have left, including drugs, and leave town.

Five days later their bodies are found in their car, ripe from the merciless sun, just outside Florence, Arizona.

Phelony Lynn, finally disbarred for failing to make monetary restitution to former clients, works in a bank.

Judge Dresden, still on the bench, teaches ethics for the state bar.

The Lawyer Cup sits behind the counter in a pawnshop a few blocks from the court house.

JUSTICE DELAYED

DEPUTY "RICH" RICHARDS PULLED UP BEHIND THE station, bag of fast food in hand, ready for a short sit down in the break room before returning to the street. His shift would be over at 7:00 a.m.

Watch Commander King marched into the room. "Rich, my man! Did ya get to fight with anybody tonight? Are ya keepin' those knuckleheads out there in line?"

Richards, used to this kind of banter from Sergeant King, peered up from the table, mouth full, then smiled. King was currently involved in a lawsuit arising from a chase in which the perpetrator suffered severe head injuries while being apprehended. King, always confident, never let anything get him down.

Clearing his palate, Rich replied, "It's been pretty quiet. A vehicle break-in, a drunk wandering through a trailer park, loud music and a distraught lady sitting outside the old Corner Drug Store." Rich sipped from his paper cup. "She was crying about being lost, so we called an ambulance to take her to the mental ward."

"Keep up the good work. Maybe this place will get us some funding so we can add more deputies and spring for some promotions." A police agency absorbed most of a municipality's budget. Counting police and fire services together, the cost could easily amount to one-fourth of all funds. Richards knew this, and he also knew that lawsuits like the one against King and the County drained the operating budget, notwithstanding municipal liability insurance.

"You got it, Sarge!" Richards said, with enthusiasm.

"Good man, Rich!" King poured himself a cup from the black and silver Bunn coffee maker, then stepped away to his office.

Just four more hours on patrol, then Rich would head home to the hills above town. His wife would be at her teaching job at the elementary school, and his two boys would be there also. His patrol area covered just over nine square miles... an area that a single deputy could cover alone, with enough help on duty if needed. The town, built on uneven geography, comprised hills, a deep wash, and brush with trees in yards that seemed to be forever in need of trimming.

Back on the road at 3:00 a.m., Rich passed by the Old Mill Creek Tavern. He rolled into the lot for a quick look around, but there were no late-night customers sleeping in their cars. Nothing but feral cats crawling over cardboard in the dumpsters. A large, faded, old Chrysler lumbered along the street heading west. Rich watched it cruise by, then nudged his car to the street. He drove from the lot in the same direction as the Chrysler, keeping a modest distance between the vehicles.

Rich passed one of the large trailer parks in town and glanced around. There were a number of them in town, all fairly close together. The residents hardly ever caused trouble except for occasional family fights or theft violations.

He looked down a side street and thought he recognized the Chrysler parked in the dark under a tree. He pulled a U-turn of his Ford Interceptor and brought it in a direct line behind the old car where he stopped. Rich ran his spotlight over the back window and into the vehicle. A couple sat in the front seat.

After switching on the Ford's red lights, Rich stepped out of the car and walked cautiously to the driver's side of the Chrysler. A young man rolled down the window.

"How are you folks doin' tonight?"

"We're doin' okay. What's up, Deputy?" The driver appeared to be about six feet, blond wavy hair, wearing a silver earring. The woman next to him had thin, graying brown hair. She wore shorts and had a crucifix dangling around her neck. They could be lovers, potential burglars, or tweekers—those who occasionally got high on speed. The time of night and dark location of the car could mean anything. Rich's senses went on high alert.

"May I see your license and registration?"

The driver handed him the documents.

"Wait here, please."

Rich returned to his Ford and ran the license and registration through the system. Both had expired. The report also showed the driver had a warrant for DUI. The license showed the driver was barely 19 years old. Rich radioed for backup and returned to the old car.

"Step out of the car, please."

"What's wrong? Is something wrong, Deputy?" The driver, wide-eyed, mouth agape, swung open the door and got out. His dirty leather jacket hung loosely from his thin frame.

"I'll tell you in a minute. Turn around and put your hands on the roof." The driver complied and Rich patted him down. "You have an outstanding warrant for a DUI."

"No!" he protested. "I took care uh that!"

Without warning, the lanky driver broke free and sprinted toward a cinder block wall separating the street from the trailer park. Rich tore after him. Just before the wall, Rich grabbed the driver by the shoulders and pulled him back. At 5 foot 8 inches, he had trouble stopping the driver. Putting one leg behind the driver, he tried to make him fall backwards. The man fell but quickly rolled to one side, scrambling toward the wall. Then, placing his hands on top of the wall, he used his feet and toes to claw his way over.

With a burst of energy, Rich leapt at the wall and hauled himself over. They fell together into thick green ivy, wrestling to gain the upper hand. But Rich was far more experienced in hand-to-hand combat, and slammed the driver with two intense distraction blows to the ribs. This slowed the man. He gasped for air as he crawled out of the bushes toward a traffic lane in the park. Out of breath, he rolled onto his back, hands raised. "No more... no more... I give up!"

"Get on your stomach," Rich growled. "On your stomach!"

The man did what he was told.

"Why did you run? You got a lot more charges now, buddy!" Rich handcuffed the driver as the wail from a siren approached the park.

Deputy Stearns pulled up behind the Interceptor, assessed the situation, and exited his vehicle. The woman from the Chrysler sat on the curb smoking a cigarette.

"Where's the other officer?"

She nodded toward the wall.

"Are you okay? Do you need any medical aid?" asked Stearns.

The woman exhaled and shook her head.

Stearns pulled himself up on the wall and peered over. Rich obviously had the situation under control. "You need medical?"

"You mean for me, or this jerk?" replied Rich, holding the driver on the ground.

The man grunted. "I need an ambulance. You broke... my ribs." This complicated matters.

Stearns radioed that medical aid would be required, and that the ambulance should respond code two—no lights or siren while entering the trailer park. Stearns questioned the woman and told her to stay with her vehicle. He drove around to the park entrance.

Rich, curious as to why the driver took off the way he did over a simple DUI warrant, searched around the cinder block wall. Within minutes, he retrieved a gun in the ivy where the struggle took place. The driver received treatment for his sore ribs from the paramedic. He denied the gun had been in his possession, insisting he didn't know where it came from. After more questioning of the man and woman, Rich determined that the driver was a member of the Steep Mountain Boys—one of the two gangs in town. The rival gang, called Little Rascals, kept the local druggies supplied with weed.

Back at the precinct, Rich charged the driver with a number of crimes, the most serious of which was possession of a concealed loaded firearm with intent to commit great bodily harm. The driver pleaded not guilty and, after a month, the matter went to a jury trial. Rich testified about the encounter with the driver and was calm and confident in his account of the facts. But the public defender, citing no evidence that Rich had actually seen the weapon in his client's possession, created a doubt reasonable enough to allow a not guilty verdict on that charge. As for the struggle with Rich and attempted escape, the driver was sentenced to six months in jail. At least the driver would be locked up during the holidays... something that gave Rich a measure of satisfaction.

Rich left the courthouse knowing that if things had gone really bad, the driver might have used the gun to escape. At the same time, he understood that guys like him always pushed their luck. He would screw up again, and when he did, Rich hoped that he would be there.

* * *

IN LATE MARCH, WHILE ON A ROUTINE PATROL, RICH bumped into the late-night driver at Bea's Coffee Shop. He'd just returned to his Interceptor with a coffee, and seated himself inside when the driver strolled across the parking lot. The two glanced at each other. The driver recognized Rich and approached him, smiling.

"Hey Deputy, how ya doin?" The driver's tone was friendly and sincere. His ashen face glowed in the light and his eyes were bloodshot. Rick recognized immediately the symptoms of drug use.

"Very good, and you?" replied Rick looking the driver in the eye.

"Ahm okay, I just got outta the slammer. I don't wanna go back there." He swayed gently on his feet.

"Behave yourself and you won't," Rich said, eyeing the man for a possible weapon.

"Yeah, I know. Say listen..." The driver looked down for a moment. "I would never use a gun on anybody, man. That night when I went over the wall, I just wanted to ditch the piece I had on me. I packed for protection, know what I mean? I'm sorry about the fight, man."

Rich's back stiffened. "So, you had the gun on you for protection from the Little Rascals?"

"Well yeah, and to impress the girl I was with."

Grinning, Rich did his best to stifle his laughter. The "girl" that young driver was with appeared to be well over forty and a meth user, which added another ten years onto her looks.

"So the gun was yours?" Rich continued.

"Yeah, man. I had an agreement to give it to one of the Boys."

"The Steep Mountain Boys? You know you're not supposed to do stuff like that." Rich kept the tone of the conversation on a *buddy buddy* level.

"Well yeah, man. I don't wanna get caught with a piece on me, man."

"Okay, thanks. Keep out of trouble, and get a job." Rich offered the man the only encouragement he could think of.

The following week, the district attorney refiled charges against the driver along with other members of the Steep Mountain Boys for theft and conspiracy to receive stolen property.

At the trial, the belt recording made by Rich during the encounter at Bea's, and brought into evidence, was enough to get a conviction against the driver and the Boys on all counts.

BLOOD WORK

"GET THE NURSE! HURRY!" PHIL HASTINGS BELLOWED and threw his arms out. He began slumping toward the counter, his eyes fluttering. I reached over, thrust my left hand on his back and my right on his chest, and eased him onto the tile floor as he slid off the stool. Other soldiers in the recovery lounge at the town blood bank rushed over.

Phil's cleaning the floor with his uniform, I thought. Luckily, he didn't crack open his shaved head. I would have laughed at him and called him a dud, but being a good roommate, I held back.

A public relations program at Fort Wolters in Texas had been set up to reduce opposition to the war in Vietnam. Our platoon was chosen to come out to a small Texas town to give blood for a little boy who had some kind of cancer. The goodwill generated would hopefully minimize the protests, and getting away from the post was always a welcome relief from the spit and polish that accompanies officer training and helicopter flight school.

Just riding out to the blood bank in a bus was a great escape from our barracks. The barracks were a gray, three-story concrete world ruled by grim-faced tactical officers and senior cadets who were always looking for something wrong with us... usually our uniforms or our rooms. Or the way our shirts hung in the closet. Socks not properly rolled. A waste basket with waste in it!

We had a sink and mirror we never used lest it be found with water or soap anywhere in or on the porcelain. Shoes and boots including the soles had to be polished. And it seemed like we never got enough sleep. But we would graduate as Warrant Officers and helicopter pilots upon completion of 36 weeks of training. One day it would all be worth it, and this was a small price to pay.

One large drawer under our closet space contained our toiletries and underwear. When we arrived at the Fort, the trainers showed us a diagram of how each item for our hygienic care was to be placed with proper distance from the drawer sides and from each other. It was comical to see that a hairbrush was required since our heads were shaved, but whatever. Ours was not to question why...

We were allowed tobacco; however, if a butt was ever found in the room or in an ashtray, there was hell to pay. At one point during training, I smoked Swisher Sweets—small cigars—as if they were cigarettes. This was due to the stress of training and cadet life.

Still, in the middle of all this madness, I looked up to our Tactical Officer, Warrant Officer Montgomery. He was stern but fair. The kind of man who easily earned respect and admiration. Some training officers returning from Vietnam had been wounded. One young man, blond hair, tall, barely 21 years old, limped along with a cane. Another, older, gruff, and built like a bouncer, wore a black leather glove over a mangled right hand. We never really saw any of this: we focused only on the glamor of earning our wings.

Before the sun rose, and before our bus ride, we donned our 1968 era khaki uniforms with carefully placed brass insignia, spit-shined shoes, dress hats, and rosy smiles. It was a special outing where we would see what the rest of Texas looked like, and we cadets were up for the occasion. We lined up for inspection outside the barracks, then Montgomery yelled, "Let's do it!" and waved his swagger stick. Heavy black boots pounded the pavement and bus floor as we took our seats.

On arrival at the blood bank—a single-story, sand-colored building—we lined up and were told to go inside in twos and threes showing a casual manner of entry. An odd-looking man wearing glasses, dark slacks, and a short-sleeve white shirt with a western bolo string tie greeted Tac Officer Montgomery. He welcomed us all and invited us inside.

After shuffling into a meeting room, we were introduced to a woman standing next to three boys. The youngest kid, about five-years-old, smiled at us as the platoon entered. His face was pale and dark circles formed under his eyes. His arms and legs were thin and bony.

We were here for him.

The woman—the kid's mom—was slim and somewhat attractive. She had long brown hair and wore faded jeans. She looked tired but grateful to see us. The family's worn clothing appeared second hand, reminding me of how challenging daily life could be for some folks.

The kid's mom shared some of her story with us... how her husband simply disappeared one night, and how she struggled as a waitress to raise her boys right. Despite the kid's poor health, he seemed happy enough and thankful we had come all the way from Fort Wolters to help him.

"I want to join the military when I grow up," he said.

We shouted our approval and his eyes widened with delight.

Following the blood collection protocol, the platoon began checking in with the nurses, and receiving tickets for comfortable padded tables. After about three hours, we'd provided 40 pints of blood.

We met again later with the family to wish them well. A hometown news photographer took pictures of us with them as we presented the boy with a model helicopter. The nurses and volunteers led us to a recovery room where we could sit and have orange juice, cookies, and coffee—the coffee that may have put my buddy Hastings on the floor.

Now Phil lay on the floor, pale as the white tile itself, catching his breath. A female attendant, dressed in white, rushed over and placed a towel under his head. She asked him questions to assess him.

"Do you know what day of the week it is?"

"How many fingers am I holding up?"

Phil soon came to his senses and opened his eyes, highly embarrassed by all the attention. The nurse told him to slow down as he tried to stand.

"I got dizzy when I put the coffee cup to my lips and barely tasted it," Phil said. He sat up, insisting on getting up by himself as he stepped back to the counter and drank some orange juice.

Later, when we returned to barracks, I didn't rib him about the incident. I was too busy changing into a fatigue uniform and squaring away my gear. Montgomery congratulated us on a job well done. One cadet, the oldest in our group at age 29, said we probably should have brought the "sick kid" a pair of shoes.

After a short meeting, Montgomery said, "Carry On!" We disbanded and studied in our rooms for the next day's training. Map reading was on the calendar, and I was overwhelmed with fatigue from the blood recovery and the family's gratitude. I couldn't stop yawning and thought about calling it a day. We always went to bed early but never seemed to get enough sleep.

★ ★ ★

ABOUT TWO WEEKS LATER, WHILE CHECKING MY MAILBOX on the first floor, I heard "Mex," a heavy set, army staff sergeant company clerk, talking to a couple of officers about the kid we gave blood for. The boy had died of leukemia during the night. Mex had been in contact with public relations and got the news that morning.

That's too bad, I thought. I ran upstairs to read my mail. There was studying to do and a room to keep clean. Floors to polish, latrines to mop, uniforms to inspect, manuals to study and keep in order, and the ever-present tac officers to watch out for.

Every now and then I think about that little kid... his short brown hair, worn striped t-shirt, faded jeans, and how happy he was to have his picture taken with us.

Carry on. Carry on.

THE LONG RIDE

ONE OF THE MOST AMBITIOUS PROJECTS EVER CONCEIVED in the American West was known simply as the Long Ride. The purpose? To deliver mail from St. Joseph, Missouri to Sacramento, California—nearly 2000 miles on horseback across the Great Plains and over the Rocky Mountains in 10 days. In 1860, The Central Overland and Pikes Peak Express Company formed a new company called the Pony Express to carry mail under contract with the federal government.

Danny Lee Brown was a boy raised on a farm in Utah by his Aunt Margaret and Uncle James. The two were not really Dan's blood relatives, and he knew this. They acquired him, for a fee, from an orphanage in Salt Lake City when he was six years old. The childless couple needed someone to help work the farm, and Dan needed a stable family to care for him.

Dan learned responsibility from an early age. He went to church, learned to read, and hunt. A tall kid, he spent most of his early years in a saddle gaining a rider's skill of boys twice his age. At times he thought of what it might be like to ride across open fields and over mountains to see the rest of the world.

While loading grain sacks one day in Kaysville, Dan saw a poster offering work with the Russell, Majors, and Waddell Freight Company. The job paid $50.00 per month for riders to carry mail from St. Joseph, Missouri, to Sacramento. The poster read that young, skinny, wiry fellows not over eighteen were needed, and that orphans were preferred. Dan's heart pounded with strong anticipation on reading the poster.

He applied without telling James or Margaret. He loved them but had grown tired of staying in one place. The first jobs with the Pony Express went to boys deranged enough to risk their lives riding nonstop over narrow trails through hostile Indian territory at all hours and in all weather. Horsemen could not tip scales at over 130 pounds.

Riders were required to take a loyalty oath, swearing that they would not use profane language, drink intoxicating liquors, or quarrel with any Express employees. They were to conduct themselves honestly and be faithful to their duties.

Dan went into the town telegraph office one day to find a message that he had been accepted into the Pony Express. He left a note for James explaining that he was grateful for taking him in and for teaching him how to be an honest man. He felt sorry to leave but he wanted to travel west and see the ocean and San Francisco someday.

He, along with two others, were taken by a freight company wagon to the Boyd Express Station in the Utah Territory on the border with Nevada. On arrival, he was issued new boots, a thick, dark blue bib-front shirt, a calf-hide bound bible and a .36 caliber revolver. Boyd Station was part cave, part rock, and part rough-hewn logs. Dan was given the care of a horse called Blue.

Blue was a Morgan, a breed developed by Thomas Morgan of Vermont in 1789. The Morgan was a strong, hardy steed originally bred for the US Cavalry. Blue was well suited for the Pony Express. The stable boy said he'd never been beaten in a log-hauling match by horses half again as heavy. Morgans were also known for their trotting speed, making them an ideal breed for the Long Ride.

Express riders originally carried two Colt revolvers, a Sharps carbine and a long blade knife. Riders found all this gear cumbersome, so they later carried one revolver with an extra cylinder loaded with extra bullets. The extra cylinder was wax coated for protection from dirt and moisture. They carried the mail in hard leather bags attached to a leather cover that fit over the saddle horn. Riders were instructed to avoid fighting if attacked. Their lives depended on the rate of speed traveled.

On his first ride, Dan waited at Boyd Station, standing next to Blue, ready to move as soon as the relay rider came in with the mail. Dan's heart quickened as he heard the rider 100 yards out. Before Dan knew it, the rider arrived in a cloud of dust. The station master grabbed the mail bag from the incoming horse and threw it onto Blue's saddle. In a flash of energy, Dan mounted Blue and took off as if propelled by a slingshot. They formed a perfect cadence as they galloped away east under the blistering sun.

On this part of the 1800-mile race against time, Dan and Blue moved together with the rhythm of a steam engine. Blue's legs flexed like pistons pounding the trail, and each stride brought the mail closer to Saint Joseph. Though arduous, the thrill of the ride lifted Dan's spirit to the point where he didn't hear anything. He felt as if he was watching someone else thundering along the hot, dusty trail.

As he neared the next outpost, Dan smelled the familiar stench of smoke carried on the wind. Then, shots cracked and echoed.

"Oh Lord," Dan yelled, "what is happening?"

A column of smoke grew thicker as he approached the outpost. He reminded himself not to slow down. If Paiute Warriors had destroyed the station, Blue would have to keep racing along no matter how exhausted.

Dan's fear was confirmed as he reached a clearing where the station had been. Only a pile of burning logs remained of the structure. The livestock was gone. As he flew past, he saw the bloodied bodies of the wrangler and station master. Dan's heart sank in his chest. He sensed Blue's nervousness, so he put spurs to the steed's side and yelled, "There's water up ahead, boy, keep going!" The next station remained 10 miles out. As they raced along the trail, Dan kept his palm on one of the revolvers.

Dan had no way of knowing at the time, but he carried an extraordinary message with him that day. Abraham Lincoln had been elected president, and stuffed in the mail bag was the State of California's response to President Lincoln's inaugural address to the nation. With trouble brewing between the Northern and Southern states, it was important for Californians to be heard in Washington. Their response could determine whether California stayed in the Union or swayed over to the Confederacy.

The sight of the destroyed station made Dan forget about the heat, sweat, dust, pain, and thirst. Though he cared for Blue, Dan would push them both to the point of collapse if necessary.

Nearly drained, they reached the next outpost without incident. The station master transferred the mail to a new horse and rider. They took off at top speed, horse hooves kicking back clods of dirt high into the air. Having done their part,

Dan and Blue could now rest. They would carry mail again in two days.

★ ★ ★

DAN EMBRACED THE HARSH LONG RIDE LIFE FOR THE eighteen months of the Pony Express, never minding extreme weather, rough terrain, or attacks by bandits and Indians. When allowed rest, he slept in basic dirt floor sheds near a horse corral. That way, he saved his pay of $50.00 per month and kept his dream alive of owning land to raise his own horses.

The last day mail was carried, the company presented Dan with saddlebags in honor of his loyal service. His initials were expertly stamped on the dark leather: DLB.

Always the adventurer, Dan joined the 29th Ohio infantry during the Civil War. On the last day of the Battle of Gettysburg, July 3, 1863, fighting raged at Culp's Hill where Union troops engaged Confederate soldiers. After seven hours of continuous conflict, Union troops forced the enemy into retreat. Danny Brown died that day at the base of the hill, having been cut down in the last hour of fighting, the day before his 17th birthday.

FREE

CREEPING THROUGH THICK BRUSH IN THE STILL OF night, uphill, was not easy. But Mario could do it. The farther he got from the camp, the better his chances of escape. The goons would be looking for him at daylight when he missed the morning formation. They would not find him this time.

He tore his thick coat wriggling under the fence, and blood warmed his back where he scraped it on the merciless metal. Still, he would not be denied. Not this time. The distant hills and mountains beyond meant the promise of a neutral country and with it the chance to go home.

He remembered the struggle to move the main camp as the Russian advance westward sent the German Army scrambling to new defensive positions. At his first stop, he and his fellow POWs—all 170 of them—were squeezed into a collapsing barn. Their welcome dinner, boiled potato peelings, was dumped from old pots onto the ground near the door. He could still see men scrambling on their knees to get a share of the muddy scraps. Not anymore. He had to make it out this time.

Every hundred yards, he stopped and cocked his ear, listening for men and dogs moving in his direction. He needed no compass. The journey uphill, over the other side where there was no war, meant he would soon be eating warm bread and cheese, with wine, and Swiss chocolate. His wife Gwen waited for him. She would be there to greet him.

★ ★ ★

LAURA BELLINI WOKE IN THE MORNING AS USUAL IN HER brightly-colored bedroom. Her mother's portrait on the wall faced the sun as it shone into the room. Another photo of her father Mario, in uniform, rested on the dresser with pictures of her adult son and daughter. Laura, divorced and living with Mario, worked part time in retail. The job offered discounts on the clothing she loved.

The only hard part of her day occurred when she brought coffee, soft boiled eggs, and toast to her father, while looking into his eyes for a hint of whether he would recognize her *this morning*. Donning her robe, she swept her hair aside, then padded into the kitchen where she began the morning ritual. This day, she decided to add some strawberry jam to the menu.

Taking a full tray down the hall toward her father's room, she smiled at the thought of seeing him. He could always be counted on to deliver a smile at the light breakfast whether he recognized her or not. She tapped on the door and pushed it open with her foot.

The bed was empty.

Thinking he must be in the bathroom, she called to him as she set the silver tray on the stand next to the bed. She opened the curtains for more light. As she surveyed the yard, she saw a pile of dirt near the chain link fence. Was it the dog? Some creature digging around?

"Dad, are you there?"

No reply came. She tapped on the bathroom door. No answer. She pushed the door open, afraid he might have fallen. He refused to use a walker or cane, unwilling to accept that arthritis with loss of balance could send him to the ER. He was a tough old guy who spoke often of his glory days in the airborne. He'd spent the last five months of the war in a POW camp in Germany.

He was not in the bathroom. Laura gasped and turned to look around the bedroom as if he might appear in the hall. No, he was definitely missing... again. She hurried to the front door. Perhaps he'd wandered out? Maybe he hadn't walked too far away? Out front she saw only a scruffy, lost dog passing by and the parched hills in the distance, brown from lack of rain.

★ ★ ★

MARIO BELIEVED HE WAS MAKING GOOD TIME. HE KNEW better than to become overconfident: the enemy was persistent. If he could just make it over the first foothill, the goons might give up looking for him and return to tend to the other prisoners.

Climbing up a steep gully, skinning his hands and knees, he refused to give up despite the pain in his bones. His training would get him through. Once he reached a neutral country, he'd get help for his buddies. He'd never abandon them.

★ ★ ★

LAURA RUSHED INSIDE THE HOUSE TO CALL THE SHERIFF'S Department. A dispatcher answered. He took down her information and agreed to send a patrol car out shortly. Laura called up a neighbor, Betty, to ask whether anyone had seen Mario.

"Oh sorry, Laura, but I haven't seen him at all. I'll put the word out to others right away."

Deputy McCauley pulled into her driveway with a ride along in tow—some young department explorer, named Quinn. Laura answered the door and invited them inside. They declined an offer of coffee or water. She took the two outside to show them the hole under the fence.

From the placement of the dirt and bend in the chain links, McCauley figured that someone had dug their way out of the yard. Laura explained that her father had been diagnosed with Alzheimer's disease and had gone missing about three times before but had always been found a few blocks away or had wandered back home on his own, bruised and dirty. The last time Mario disappeared, he'd gone over the five-foot fence using a step stool taken from the garage. This left him with bruises and a swollen cheek when he landed on the other side.

McCauley called dispatch on his radio and requested a search and rescue unit the department kept on call. These SAR volunteers had special expertise. A rescue leader would conduct a search if Mario had not been found in the next two hours. His Alzheimer's made this a special case.

Laura believed her father would be found again, but that didn't stop her from worrying.

★ ★ ★

WHEN THERE WAS STILL NO SIGN OF MARIO AFTER A couple of hours, a citizen volunteer, Corporal Sands, appeared at Laura's door. She recognized him from the last time Mario had gone missing, and explained the current situation to him. Sands recalled the last time that they'd found Mario late in the evening, a block from the house. His arms and knees were skinned up, and his nose had bled. He had someone's mail with him delivered the same day to an address almost a mile away. Mario had taken it for no reason he could explain.

Sands, hoping for a quick resolution, decided to ask Deputy McCauley to let Quinn help with the search. McCauley agreed. Sands and Quinn drove through the area in Sands' truck. The two kept in touch with dispatch via Sands' handheld radio. A larger search would call for more volunteers, something Sands did not believe would be necessary... not yet at any rate.

Close to ninety percent of those with Alzheimer's are found within one-half to a mile from home. About three-quarters of them had a history of wandering. Sands knew that if Mario was found in twelve hours, everything would be okay, barring some serious injury. If he was not found in three days, chances are they would not find him alive.

★ ★ ★

DARKNESS SET IN. STILL NO SIGN OF THE GOONS.

Mario felt refreshed as a cold wind brushed against his face. It invigorated him. Though hungry and thirsty, Mario felt cleansed of the filthy barn, its horrific smell, and the fear that the camp goons might set fire to it before abandoning him and the other men. Believing that he had picked the best escape route uphill, he continued. All he had to do was stay low and keep moving, keep moving. Nothing would stop him this time.

★ ★ ★

ON THE AFTERNOON OF THE THIRD DAY, AFTER FLYERS with Mario's picture and Laura's phone number had been posted throughout the neighborhood, the search continued with no luck, no clues as to the man's whereabouts. On the fifth day, the Sheriff's Department had issued a BOLO for Mario. Sands and his expanded crew of volunteers plus boy scouts had marched over hills, through brushland, and searched alleys and dumpsters. They'd contacted street people and launched small drones.

Nothing.

The entire effort slowed. Laura prayed that her father would be found. She would not give up believing.

But a man with a solid mindset to avoid capture will not be found.

After seven months, in late December, while hiking after a light snowfall in high elevation, a young woman (coincidentally named Laura) along with her boyfriend found what looked like tattered remains of a sleeping bag in a deep narrow gully off the trail.

Forensic experts identified the remains.

Staff Sergeant Mario Bellini was buried with full military honors alongside his wife Gwen shortly after. Unhampered by a confused mind, Mario Bellini was finally free.

DAUNTING TIMES

Friday night at the house was always full of anticipation. While every night could bring a gathering of friends, a person could count on weekends for special excitement. The guys had planned a birthday party for their roommate, Matt, on Saturday.

Four young guys rented the place—a clean, wood frame, ranch house on the edge of town. Matt, Nick, and Gene were junior college students. Cole, the ladies' man, drove a market delivery truck. He was the only one who earned money. The rest lived on their G.I. Bill checks, their reward for going on an all-expense paid trip to Southeast Asia in the late 1960s.

Short school days left them lots of time to hang out, watch TV, and drink beer. Matt brought over a full-size pool table from his folk's house which they set up in the garage. He also plugged in a bone-rattling sound system there. It supplied a special thrill to hear *Smoke On The Water* by Deep Purple, or *Do It Again* by Steely Dan.

It was a party house, but a relatively quiet one on a short section of the street next to a meadow and a wash that became a deep stream when it rained. Four bedrooms, two baths, and a large green backyard made life here just about perfect. At Christmas, they decorated the fireplace with help from the girls who came over. They usually studied either at the college library or the kitchen table.

Cole had a beautiful young girlfriend, shapely with long dark hair, named Janet. Though he was a lucky guy, the luckiest in fact, he rented the place with the rest of the guys so that he could bring other girls to the house. Cole's lot was the result of an unhappy marriage and divorce that left him with a four-year-old daughter. Little Mary lived in Tidelands with her mother, an attractive woman herself, somewhat older than Janet.

Matt wanted to paint his old 1962 Austin Healy. Gene got friends to pitch in with cash for the paint job, and he and Nick stuffed some money in an old bank deposit bag they found in a thrift shop. The presentation would be a nice touch.

Matt was ready to party. His cake was in the fridge, along with tall cans of Coors. He would provide some weed, too. Just one more day.

★ ★ ★

LATER THAT NIGHT WHEN MATT AND GENE WERE watching Kung Fu on TV, they noticed headlights swing along the gravel driveway. Matt stretched and got up, then peered through a curtain. He turned back sharply, his mouth open with eyes bulging as if he had bitten into a red-hot pepper.

"There's... there's a cop car in the driveway!" he gasped. Its lights flashed against the wall.

Gene jumped up. This was not a joke. There was weed in the house!

Matt raced to the hallway, turning, then returning with a paper grocery bag. Gene held his hands to his forehead. They panicked, babbling, until finally they made a plan to clear the house of what could send them to jail.

They grabbed all the weed from their normal hiding places, and stuffed it in the bag. Gene took the bag of weed out the back door to stash it in the field behind the house.

He flew over the back wall and ran. Gene stumbled through the dark toward brush that was three and four feet tall. He tossed the bag behind some shrubs and kept running farther through the field. He stopped to catch his breath and turned to look at the distance he had covered. The only sound he heard was the incessant pounding of his heart. Wouldn't there be some noise if the cops showed up in force to raid the house? He sank to his knees, gasping for air.

Gene had no idea there was so much weed in the house. The paper bag held about a pound, he figured. More than enough to get him and the others in some serious trouble.

Time to regroup. The best thing would be to appear as if he had not been at the house, and just walk home normally. But he wanted to spend some time away from the trouble. Shaking, inhaling deeply, he could walk toward the lights of Blakes Liquor Store way around the corner. But what then? He decided to figure it out during the walk. Often, in the war, they had to improvise and make things up as they went. If he could do it there and survive, he could certainly do it here. He made his way along the edge of the field to the street.

The store had everything the guys liked. Beer, wine, soda, girlie magazines, junk food, candy, Marlboros. The place was a guy magnet.

Lights grew brighter as he approached the store, so he stayed in the shadows. The mom and pop grocery across the street was closed. He decided to go behind Blakes to sit on the dirty wooden crates the old man stored there. He lit a cigarette in the dark and gazed out over a clearing behind the store toward some old flat-roof homes on the other side of a storm drain some distance away. A sweaty itchiness set in on his neck and shoulders. He listened to the night sounds, but everything remained still, quiet and dark. What if they were looking for him? What happened to Matt? Oh God. Was he arrested?

What have we done? Gene thought about his friends and family. What would his family think? He had been in jail once in San Francisco. That was for theft, but the charge was dropped. It turned out that someone who looked like Gene robbed a man in Golden Gate Park. Still, it took more than two days to get out of City Prison. He went to court later where a rude, overbearing female judge ordered him to pay a fine for loitering and to stay away from the park.

Gene flicked his cigarette butt away and dropped his head. A car pulled into the parking lot. A door slammed. Someone spoke in Spanish. What if they robbed the place and Gene was found behind the store? No. That would not happen. He hopped off the crates.

He knew he would have to return to the house sooner or later. Better make it sooner. He might have to take his medicine. Gene strolled to the front of the store and looked down the street. Nothing unusual appeared. No lights or commotion. He turned toward a phone booth and stared at it. Who would answer if he called the house?

"This never should have happened," Gene said to himself, keeping his nerve. This was real, not a dream. Should he start praying? Would he? Religion made guilt a virtue, his father once said.

He found himself inside the corner phone booth. A dime could at least shed light on what was happening. Suddenly, a small man appeared outside the booth... a disgusting bum in worn, dirty shoes. A black crust adorned his coat collar. He tapped on the booth glass with one hand as he held the other out. His face shone like a rusted tin roof, and he smiled through tobacco-stained teeth—at least what was left of them.

Startled, Gene turned away. The little man moved around to the other side of the booth, looking at Gene in the eye. Is this a joke? That's it, God is playing a joke. He raised his face to the sky. "Is this really what I want?" The bum shuffled off and Gene continued. "Oh please let me change this." As he spoke, the tension building up in his body and mind released. He squeezed his eyes shut and made a resolution.

Seconds later, Gene decided to call. After dropping a dime into the phone, he dialed. The phone rang and rang. Did they take Matt away? Someone answered. It was Matt!

"Where are you, Gene? Everything's okay here... come back to the house."

Gene wanted assurance. Was someone forcing Matt to say that?

"Everything is fine," Matt insisted, "no one else is at the house."

Gene opened the booth door, made sure the bum was gone, and set out toward the house. The walk home was not lit by any street or porch lights. At least no dogs barked, and Gene was glad of that. For a while, he thought about leaving the guys to get a place by himself. He could move out and still enjoy life. Just have a bit more control.

He arrived at the side door in between the garage and large kitchen. It was unlocked. Matt sat at the table, drinking a Pepsi. Gene entered and helped himself to a Coors. He sat across from Matt. "What the hell happened?"

Matt smiled and explained that Judy Fisher had stopped by with a city cop right behind her. Tall, pretty, long dark hair, with a seemingly constant serious look, she could be found at a nightclub on occasion doing shots when downers were not available. She liked to hang out with bikers. Gene once saw her reach into her jeans to retrieve a baggie of red pills from her crotch.

"The cop followed Judy into the driveway because she ran the stop sign at the corner near Blakes Liquor," Matt said. "He told her to step out of the car and empty her pockets. It had nothing to do with us."

Matt and Gene agreed there was no reason for the cop to do this. Clearly unlawful, they mused. The cop found a downer among some breath mints, change, and a match book.

"The guy told her he'd give her a break if she dropped the red capsule onto the driveway and grinded it down. She did so with her boot." He sipped his Pepsi. "Judy, always cool and charming, thanked the cop the way she does, then came inside and asked for a drink."

Gene shook his head. Matt asked where he ended up going, and he explained what he went through to protect the homestead, including his anxious mental state nearly overtaking him while down the street. He and Matt sat quietly, avoiding looking at each other.

"We can't keep doing this, Matt. I can't keep doing this." Gene leaned back in his chair.

A few minutes later, after serious discussion, they agreed to retrieve the grocery bag from the field in the morning, and when they found it, they'd get rid of it one way or another.

The future didn't have to include the risks they took. "It's just not worth it," Gene said.

Matt looked around the kitchen. "You're right, Gene." He put his head down, then rubbed the back of his neck.

They decided that no more dope was allowed in the house. Judy could be trouble for all who lived there. She wouldn't be told to stay away but she would have to call first before coming over, and she could never bring any kind of drug with her. New house rules.

Meanwhile, life would go on at the house, cleanly, with purpose, without unlawful risks.

Gene finished his beer. Peace settled over him. He could even see himself, with help, graduating junior college and going on to a four-year school. He calmed himself, smiled, and saw a teaching degree in his future.

TEAM WORK

"HERE WE ARE, SIR... FILET MIGNON, MEDIUM RARE, WITH creamed spinach, and sauteed mushrooms... green beans with wild hot cheese." The waiter wore short sleeves with a red top hat. "Would you like some cold Kool-Aid?"

Tom gazed at the woman across the table. Her blond hair rose from her head in the tallest beehive style. She smiled and served herself thick oatmeal from a huge wood bowl.

"You're not saying anything," she said in a low voice.

Looking at the six martini glasses on the table, Tom said, "You are so pretty."

★ ★ ★

THE ALARM SHOCKED HIM AWAKE. OPENING HIS EYES, HE bolted straight up. Blaring high and low screaming tones bounced off the smooth bedroom walls. The engine crew shoved their feet into black rubber boots and pulled yellow canvas turnouts up by thick suspenders. They scrambled onto the engine room floor in 10 seconds.

A dispatcher's voice echoed through the room, informing all stations of the situation. "Engines 1 and 2, Truck 1, Battalion 1 out to 1177 Canal Street. Structure fire. Time of dispatch zero two forty hours."

Captain Taggart received more detailed information by telephone at the counter next to the engine. He nodded, slammed the phone down and jumped into his seat next to Engineer Smith. "Okay, I have it!" he said.

The engineer, groggy and sleepy-eyed, asked Taggart, "Ahh...where we goin', Tag?" He rubbed his eyes and fired up the Cummins diesel engine. The rumbling sound caused Engineer Smith to sit up straight, suddenly alert.

"Canal Street. You know where that is," Taggart responded. Since working with Engineer Smith, or "Smitty" as he was called, Taggart knew things had to be kept short and simple.

Tom dropped into his seat on the engine, resting his back against a Scott Air Pak—a self-contained breathing apparatus like a scuba diver's tank. He pulled the shoulder straps on. Then, buckling the waist belt and opening the air valve, the device hissed to life. Standard procedure called for use of the Scott Pak. Thrilled, Tom anticipated doing some "smoke diving" at the fire. If Engine 2 arrived there first, he would "catch the plug," securing an additional water source for the fire if it was a large one. The water in the engine's tank might not be enough.

As the engine eased out from the station, the automatic doors closed behind.

"No traffic at this hour... good," said Smith. "I'm waking up now."

"Well, that's good to hear!" replied Captain Taggart. "We'll need you awake if it's a Condition B."

The designation—Condition B—meant that more than the 500 gallons on the engine would be needed to handle any flames. Taggart, grabbing his map book, began the task of looking up the Canal Street area and the location of nearby hydrants. Someone had smeared the subject page with dirt and grease.

"Dammit, doesn't anybody know how to wash their hands? I can barely see this!" He flipped pages as he spoke. "You know where we're going, right?"

"Yeah," said Smitty, not exactly sure of the way. The siren screamed in the night as a few lonesome cars pulled over to the side. "Anybody out at this hour is driving drunk."

After confirming the way to Canal Street with Taggart, Smitty held his breath as an ominous glow appeared northeast of them. Acrid smoke filled the air as all three looked toward the fire.

Taggart grabbed the radio mic and called all units. "From where we are, this structure looks like it's fully involved."

The radio squelched and crackled. "Battalion 1, copy."

The chief was farthest away from the blaze, but could make better time driving a new, deep red, '75 Ford. Most of the city's 10 engines were 1963 Seagraves. They all leaked water from their 500-gallon booster tanks. Only one had a roof on it, made from fiberglass and installed at the city yard. The idea behind roofless manufactured engines was to allow the captain to stand, as a conquering guide, pointing the way to the rescue. But with or without a roof, these engines were never built for comfort.

Tom licked his lips in anticipation of heading into action. He lived in a quiet studio apartment over a mom-and-pop store on the east side of town, and enjoyed cooking for himself and hosting occasional guests while watching his TV in the kitchen. He loved his job. As "hoseman" on the fire engine, his responsibility during a call included rescue, providing first aid, and firefighting using the equipment on the engine. All this had to be accomplished by strictly following commands and procedures. He was grateful to be living the best time of his young life.

He liked bringing girls up to his place every now and then after an evening of night clubbing, too. Sometimes he shared his experiences with the other firemen. Captain O'Brien from Station 1 told Tom that he could be promoted to Engineer soon if he kept up his good work.

Nearing the burning house, Smitty slowed down to catch a hydrant. The only one they could see on a nearby corner was painted red. Not good. The color indicated that water pressure was very low, maybe under 300 gallons per minute flow. One thousand or fifteen hundred would have been far more effective. Still, the 300 was better than nothing. This part of the city didn't warrant much spending on infrastructure by the city council.

Smitty slowed the Seagraves, then stopped 15 feet past the hydrant. Tom sprang into action. He jumped down from his rear facing seat and ran to the back of the engine. Stepping up on the tailboard, he grabbed the end of the 2 ½ inch wide hose, dragging it off the hose bed and pulling enough out to reach and wrap around the hydrant. Bracing his foot on the hose, he signaled with two open hands for Smitty to move out to the fire. The hose peeled off the bed as the engine drove on.

A spanner wrench, attached to the hose, gave Tom what he needed to remove the side cap from the hydrant. After removing the cap, he connected the hose to the hydrant, but he was unable to turn on the water with the spanner.

He straightened his helmet. Someone had removed the large brass nut on top of the hydrant to sell for scrap. Tom grabbed a pipe wrench and managed to get enough of a bite on the top to get the water flowing. The wrench, fortunately, was also attached to the hose end for such situations.

Smitty eased up to a point near the flames, stopped, and pulled a red knob to set the air brakes. A loud two-second hiss followed. He jumped off his seat with the engine now secured. After scrambling to the back of the vehicle, he put a heavy clamp on the hose to stop the flow to the engine from the hydrant. He pulled hose from the engine bed and uncoupled a section, then connected it to an intake on the engine and removed the hose clamp. Smitty shifted his attention to the engine pump control panel, opened the necessary valves and checked the water pressure. All this unfolded like clockwork.

Captain Taggart, pulling hose off the engine which was connected to an engine pipe, moved toward the house, ducking his head low to avoid the heat. Smitty pulled the necessary valves, charging the hose Taggart held. A full stream of water shot out.

Tom confirmed the hydrant connection was secure, and raced to the house. As he reached the structure, Taggart shouted, "Tom, put on your mask and go see if anyone is inside!" Taggart wrestled more hose off the engine. "I'll send you some help as soon as it gets here."

Flames and smoke boiled over the house. Neighbors in pajamas, robes, and underwear, gathered on the curb and along the dark street. One man yelled, "The place is vacant! If there are any fools inside, leave 'em there! Damn junkies!" The rest of the crowd remained silent, as if watching TV... not that they'd never seen excitement on the street—ambulance crews routinely responded to medical calls, shootings, beatings, and drug overdoses in this neighborhood. But a blaze like this was a rare occurrence.

Arriving at the front door, Tom pulled on his air mask. He shoved the door open and stepped inside. Thick smoke prevented any clear sight. He dropped to his hands and knees, waving his flashlight around, and keeping his left shoulder against the wall. This technique would prevent him from getting lost in case he had to exit quickly from the blinding, smoke-filled house. If he had to scramble, he would turn around and put his right shoulder against the wall and get out.

Shouts from the outside floated in through the inferno. Other crews had arrived. He paused as flames licked the ceiling. They had already consumed the rear area of the house, along with the small back porch.

Someone approached from behind. One of the ladder truck crew. "Is there anyone in here?"

Tom barely heard the muffled voice underneath the air mask. He yelled, "I haven't found anything!"

A few seconds later, he bumped into something heavy enough to stop the forward movement of his gloved hands. Shining his flashlight on the bulky mass, he could see a zipper. A victim wearing a thick ski jacket. "Help me drag this guy out!" he yelled to his companion.

"What have you got?"

"Someone in a heavy coat... help me drag 'em to the door!"

The two lurched toward the door, past empty cans, bottles, rags, and fast food remains. Nearing the doorway, the mass appeared to be a body wrapped in thick blankets. As they burst from the door into the cooler night air, Tom pulled his mask off and cleared his throat. With sweat rolling off his face, he shouted, "Wherze zah paramedics?" Two men raced forward with a resuscitator and first aid bags.

The two attendants placed their hands on the unwieldy "coat", moving their gloved hands over partially melted nylon. After inspecting the heap for a few seconds, they suddenly looked at each other grinning, as if they had just received a promotion with a months' vacation. The bigger of the two said, "I guess your wheels are spinning, but the hamster is dead!" They howled with laughter. The noise made others think someone was in distress.

"You guys just saved a sleeping bag stuffed with trash!"

The Truckee, still on his knees, punched Tom in the shoulder, stood, and said, "This one's all yours, Tommy boy!"

As the Truckee and the paramedics left the porch, Tom pushed the bag off the edge of the landing, partly to clear the way, and partly to get the bag out of immediate sight.

Then he started laughing from deep within his gut.

★ ★ ★

THE CREWS TACKLED THE BLAZE AGGRESSIVELY. THE truck crew vented the roof, and the engine finally put enough water on the fire to knock it down and out. With low water pressure and delayed arrival by other crews, little remained of the house to salvage. The smoke cleared. At the back of the structure, black, charred wood that had been load-bearing 2x4s pointed in all directions, like a mosaic thoughtlessly tossed together through wisps of smoke and steam.

With the fire out, overhaul was the next priority. Some men sprayed small amounts of water on smoldering areas, while moving remaining hot embers around with hooks to cool them down. Other crews hauled equipment back to their engines, then talked about what was learned from the call.

As daylight brightened the street, an old, dull red, army surplus 3 / 4 ton truck pulled onto the scene, its brakes sounding like heavy chain dragged across a concrete floor. One could almost read the faded words on the door: Walkerville Fire Department. The city fathers thought the vehicle, an old army truck, was a good buy at auction in 1949 as a utility carrier. It was not the prettiest, quietest vehicle. As fire crews loaded wet hose from the fire onto the engine, a fire prevention officer in a clean white shirt stepped out of the surplus truck, his gold badge gleaming. He reached into the truck and grabbed a shiny white helmet and put it on his head. He then placed his hands on his hips and surveyed the area.

Captain Taggart approached the man. He grinned and saluted. "It's all yours now. Ready for investigation, Officer Watts."

Watts had become an investigator after ruining his knee at a nasty fire several years ago. He returned to fire suppression after some treatment but later, while crawling about in a smoke-filled warehouse, the sharp end of a five-inch nail sticking through the floor finished what was left of the tissue in the articular cartilage near his kneecap. He'd pulled it out and kept crawling on adrenaline and fear.

Walking with a limp, he said, "Okay, I got it. Thanks y'all fur comin' out." He hiked up his pants, tucked his shirt, then stroked a huge, thick, gray mustache.

Taggart's crew went to Station 1 for new, clean hose and to visit with others there. Tag, Smitty, and Tom later returned to their own station. While having coffee, their relief crew arrived. They shared the story of the house fire, their strategy, and the lessons learned... something they did after every blaze.

Tom wondered how long it would take for the matter of the sleeping bag to come up. He thought of telling it himself, but that would deprive Tag and Smitty of their fun.

"Hey, you know Tommy saved a sleeping bag at the fire this morning," Tag said. The three relief crew members at the kitchen table stopped sipping coffee to lean forward and listen. "We didn't keep it though. It was dirty, nasty, full uh trash." Tag recounted the story, adding all kinds of extra details, turning it into a tale of mythical proportions. Laughter filled the station. "You shudda seen him doing CPR on the thing!" They didn't stop laughing for a long time. It was a really good way to start the day and to release any remaining tension from fighting the fire.

One guy wiped tears of laughter from his eyes and said, "So, you're our bagman!"

Another guy jumped in. "Maybe we should call him Sleepy, like the seven dwarfs!" More laughter. "You should just let sleeping bags lie Tommy."

Tom joined in, knowing what would happen. "Well, see, I was hired before the county had a fire academy." More laughter. He knew the story would make the rounds of county stations by the late afternoon. Such was the nature of the job. Always best to go along with it, but not let anyone have too much fun or a nickname might stick. He recalled some of the legendary practical jokes he'd heard about. Like the time when all crews were at the station and sent for some pizza. Engineer Robbins, "The Grouch", demanded his pizza with everything. Returning from the engine room, he found his plate of pickles, granola, mustard, tabasco, a raw potato, and whipped cream with a cigarette on top, covering the pizza underneath. When he saw it, he just shook his head while the crew chimed, "You said you wanted everything!"

Tag got up with his coffee, then went to his office to write up the fire report. Smitty and Tom briefed the relief crew on the engine status. Clean hose, booster tank refilled, air bottles squared away.

It was now up to the new guys on shift to keep the city safe.

Tom clocked out and climbed into his car. He unwrapped a Three Musketeers bar and took a bite. He turned the ignition on his new pickup truck, hardly able to wait coming back in 24 hours and going to work again.

TRENCH GUNS

"WAKE UP YOU LAZY ASSES!" SERGEANT WICK'S VOICE boomed like a sledgehammer hitting an empty oil drum. "You too, Sandy!"

"Okay! Okay, Sarge!" I bolted up. "You don't like me very much, do ya? We're both in the same army, gimme a break."

Most of the troops were already awake, savoring the cool protection of a bunker as the sun rose over An Tan Bridge and the town of the same name. An Tan was called a village, though some buildings were constructed from concrete blocks and the main road was paved.

Unlike others who'd been drafted, I volunteered for the infantry. My friends back home told others that I left to get away from a bad family life, or maybe because my high school sweetheart moved out of state with another guy. But it wasn't like that at all.

I wanted to be a radio disk jockey or a cop—I didn't know which one at the time. The day I turned 19, I found myself at the recruiter's office. Next thing, I'm in Louisiana, training at Fort Polk...

"What time is breakfast served?" Lester asked. He was a stocky black kid from the roughest part of Chicago—a reliable trooper who once caught a bullet in his flak jacket. He held his armpit while complaining of a burning sensation. Wiggling his shoulder and removing the vest, he managed to work an AK round out of the green plastic material. He wore the bullet around his neck telling everyone that it was the one with his name on it; therefore, he could go home without ever being wounded. He liked to be called "Tonto."

* * *

A WEEK EARLIER, THE PLATOON LEFT THE FIELD TO TAKE responsibility for guarding the An Tan Bridge, or more to the point, what was left of it. Originally a railroad crossing, half of the steel trestle now rested at a downward angle in the river. The other half, refusing to give up its hold on the opposite bank, likewise slumped in the water. Duty here was good, all things considered. No crossing rivers and streams infested with leeches; no snakes, or sleeping in a hole that could become a grave.

Yes, this was easy duty. Easy money, we called it. The Corps of Engineers constructed a pontoon bridge for daily use next to the destroyed train crossing. The green pontoons were metal, resembling canoes resting sideways under the floating structure. The Vietnamese and American military used the pontoon bridge all day, along with civilians.

A two-story sandbagged tower overlooked the west side of the river. Another bunker, used as living quarters, stood near the far side of the road. Transistor radios tuned to Armed Forces Radio provided our daily entertainment.

Bridge traffic consisted of jeeps, trucks, and mobile artillery along with civilians on bicycles or pulling hand carts. Sometimes I waved to fellow troops passing by. Weather could change in minutes here. Streams of sweat poured down my face and chest most days.

We wrote letters without worrying that they would be destroyed by rain or a bath in a waist high stream before being sent. Working field phones allowed us to talk to each other at night in different bunkers.

★ ★ ★

I STRETCHED, STOOD UP, GRABBED MY CANTEEN, THEN drank cool water, chilled during the night. The bunker had four gunport openings plus an entrance just large enough for one man to pass at a time.

Doc Wilkins was out first. He always slept with his boots on. Doc was a nice guy, soft-spoken, easy to get along with... a bright guy who kept all his gear in order. He was a former university student, and no one could guess how he got here. While in a rear area, he filled some of his small medicine bottles with liquor, then placed them in his medical bag.

I stepped outside, followed by Jasper the Hillbilly. He rose to his full height, about 6'3". A brown-haired gentle giant from Oklahoma, with the emotional make up of a 12-year-old. Amiable enough. Some guys teased him, but not past a certain point. He once told me that back home there "was guys" who would cut a man's throat for just looking at a man's wife. When in the field, Jasper carried a heavy machine gun loaded with a belt of 50 rounds.

Nesmith, baby-faced, blond, of medium height, lit a cigarette first thing.

"Aren't you going to have coffee with that?" I asked. Nesmith was a Mormon and he could live on cigarettes and coffee. Joining the army gave him the chance to enjoy these vices.

"No," he replied, "today, I'll have it with beer." He took a heavy drag, exhaled, then said, "I should be gettin' some love letters today." He loved to brag about his girlfriends back home.

The locals would be out soon selling beer and sodas. With the bunker exit complete, the men gazed across the road to the tower on the other side. Sergeant Stauder, a squad leader, waved and held up a canteen cup, inviting the men over for coffee made in an old pot, cooked over a fire in a makeshift BBQ. Stauder had been a college wrestler for a time. His nickname was Ivan.

I decided to heat up some canned ham rations over a tin can burner. A burning Trioxane tab with its bluish flame heated the ham to a juicy, salty, satisfying plate. I pulled a plastic fork from my chest pocket, stabbed a slice, then began eating. This was the perfect first meal of the day.

Most of the day was spent washing up, cleaning weapons, gabbing with the locals—many of whom spoke English—and reading or writing letters home. Two men were picked to cross over into An Tan to direct traffic during the day.

A 2 ½ ton truck, called a Deuce and a Half, came by just after noon with a hot meal—spaghetti. There was milk and bread also. Clerks handed out paper plates along with forks. Some of the guys kept hot sauce or catsup, sent from home, to spice up a meal.

I lit a smoke after lunch. Marlboros were coveted over Winston. Then came Kent, then Parliament. The army supplied these along with assorted candies, in an "SP Pack," a cubic foot box of goodies.

★ ★ ★

THE WINCHESTER MODEL 1897 TRENCH GUN WAS A militarized version of a riot gun. The Great War transformed one of America's most popular sporting arms, the shotgun, into a weapon for close combat, specifically for fighting in the trenches. The military version, with a 20" barrel, 12-gauge, exposed hammer, and holding five rounds had a special feature allowing it to be "slam fired", meaning that by holding the trigger down it could be fired each time the slide was pumped. A heat shield covered the top of the barrel to protect the hand in case the weapon was used with a bayonet. It could accommodate a 15-inch blade—something one hoped would never have to be used.

Wick called a meeting in the late afternoon by way of a field phone. He emerged from the tower bunker. With hands on his hips, he said he heard that some of the guys had been getting letters from Danny Ortega's mother. Danny had written home about his tour, his job, and about some of the guys. One day he stepped on a mine cobbled together from two grenades. He died the next day in a rear area hospital.

"You guys can answer if you want to," Sergeant Wick said. "It's okay if his mother wants to pretend that her son is still alive here." Running his hand over his head, he added, "Be right back." He turned and entered the bunker.

Puzzled, we looked at each other. "Whuh, dee have to take a piss?" Nesmith said.

Wick returned with what looked like chopsticks. He cleared his throat. "Higher higher has informed us, by radio, that they're concerned about VC sappers trying to blow up the bridge here. They believe VC will try swimming in from upriver with explosives to destroy the pontoon bridge and stop construction of a permanent one."

He inhaled deeply. "Tonight, someone will have to go out over the pontoon and drop grenades into the river in case there are sappers in the water."

Tonto lit a cigarette. "Who that gonna be?" He took a long drag, exhaling upward.

"That's what these are for," Wick said, holding the sticks up. "The three newest in country will draw for the honor. Short straw goes out tonight."

The three would be me, Tonto, or Nesmith.

"Okay you guys, step forward." Wick was in a hurry to get it over with before we mounted a protest against him for the order from headquarters.

Me and Tonto stepped towards Wick. I looked at Nesmith. "Don't be shy," I said. "You can tell the girls back home how you saved the An Tan Bridge."

Wick glanced at Nesmith. "Come on, don't waste time. We got a war to win." He held out the three straws with both hands.

Tonto drew the first straw. Six inches long. He would be staying in a bunker or doing guard duty just outside. Nesmith and I looked at each other.

"Go ahead," I said. Nesmith frowned as he rubbed his thumb and index finger together. Then he drew a long straw.

"Sonofabitch!" I took the short straw.

"You get tuh save da bridge," Tonto said.

Wick stepped closer to me. "Take the trench gun, Sandy. We'll make sure you have some grenades." He dropped his hand on my shoulder. Such a fatherly blessing.

★ ★ ★

LATER THAT EVENING, AS LONG SHADOWS CREPT OVER the area, Sergeant Wick found me eating the last meal of the day, a LRRP, short for Long Range Recon Patrol meal. Add hot water to the pouch and in five minutes you get red beans, sauce, and chicken with rice.

"Hey Sandy, I have a present for you." Wick held out our trench gun. "It's all loaded. How many more shells do you want?"

"Twenty more."

"Here you go," Wick said. I stuffed them in the side pockets of my green pants. "It'll be okay. We'll be lookin' out for you, Sandy."

Taking the gun, I felt safe and reassured. With polished wood stock and fore-end, a dull black barrel, the gun was a work of art.

"How many grenades you got?"

"I have two," I said.

"I'll get you eight more. All you gotta do is pull the pin and drop 'em in the water. You'll cross over and back four times tonight."

My jaw dropped. "What? I thought it would just be over and back... like once."

"It won't be bad," Wick grinned. "We'll be watching from this side. Nothing ever happens here at night, right?"

The words meant nothing.

★ ★ ★

AN HOUR AFTER DARK, I PREPARED TO CROSS. AFTER
downing a cup of water, I used the field phone to put the word
out that I would be crossing. Gripping my weapon, I walked
fifty feet to the start of the wood and steel bridge that was
under construction. I stepped to the other side on the planks
of the incomplete span, 60 meters across. The moon shone
bright enough to see An Tan clearly, along with the shape of
the wrecked metal bridge girders.

I finally made it across the damaged section without
incident, and turned toward the pontoons. Now the real work
began. With my senses heightened, the sounds of night insects
seemed louder than usual. I got down on one knee, set the gun
down and reached into my canvas shoulder bag. Then I pulled
out a grenade.

The fragmentation grenade with explosives in its center
is wrapped with notched, thick wire inside a casing. Gripping
the grenade with my right hand, thumb over the "spoon"
which holds a spring-loaded striker over the blasting cap, I
pulled the circular pin from the grenade.

I dropped it into the water between two metal pontoons.
I waited five seconds and—*Whomp!* Such a terrible sound
below water. I glanced at the An Tan side, scanning for any
kind of possible enemy activity. Nothing yet. I stood and took
a few more steps, then dropped another.

Whomp!

As I carefully traversed the pontoon bridge, the whole
thing felt unreal. Dreamlike. Next stop was halfway across.
Another grenade. Another *Whomp!* I told myself to keep it
simple: get up, walk, and get it over.

At the next stop, I kneeled to deliver a concussion to whoever might be under the bridge. I decided to "cook off" the grenade. I released the spoon, then counted two seconds before I let the spoon fly. I dropped it about a foot over the water. Since the grenade was made with a five second delay, it sank for three seconds before detonating. Along with the deep, muffled explosion, I also heard the tinny sound of metal on metal. Some of the shrapnel reached the underside of the steel pontoons. No damage was done, fortunately.

One more stop.

Here, sweat poured off my face and my knees almost buckled. I didn't kneel. After slinging the gun over my shoulder, I tossed the grenade in the water and walked the distance back to the tower bunker.

Everyone in the tower was asleep except for Tonto. I climbed the wood ladder and found him staring out over the river, holding a canteen cup. "Hey man, you want some coffee?" Tonto said.

"No thanks," I said. "I just wanna get this patrol over and get some sleep."

Tonto offered a cigarette. I took it. We engaged in banter over bridge duty. "Can't beat dis," Tonto said. "Get to write home when we want, eat when we want, no humpin' da bush."

"Yeah, it's great if you don't have to cross An Tan Bridge at night."

"I'll walk it if day tell me to." Tonto drank some coffee. "Long as dis gun is up here." He patted the top of the M-60 Machine Gun, connected to a cable and hanging from a rafter, the gun provided all directions coverage.

Half an hour later, I figured it was time to cross again. Other than the insects, the only other sound was a distant helicopter and a strange, occasional cry from some kind of bird. I told Tonto I would see him later, and left the bunker. I climbed down the makeshift ladder to the ground, and decided not to take the same path back just in case. I set out toward the pontoon crossing.

Moonlight bathed the water as I stepped onto the bridge. Slow water, so quiet. When I reached the middle, I heard a splash.

I froze.

Raising the gun to my shoulder, I strained to hear more sounds, but the noise stopped. In less than a minute, I knelt and dropped two grenades between pontoons and waited. *Whomp! Whomp!* No blood appeared. Nothing rose to the surface, floating in the water. Nothing.

With gun at the ready, I crept to the An Tan side. Wasting no time, turning, I made it to the unfinished steel bridge. My flak jacket gave me some comfort. Adrenaline coursed through me.

Now for the walk back. I breathed deeply, scanning the water and the bridge for any kind of movement.

Nothing.

I started back over the pontoon bridge.

Quick drops. Two underwater explosions. The walk was done.

After reaching the other side, I fast-walked in the dark to the small bunker. Sweat dripped into my eyes and I wiped it away. My breath was shallow and hurried. I thought I was almost there, but with the thick shadows, it was impossible to tell accurately.

Then an unmistakable odor.

I could see Crazy Brian puffing as he sat atop the bunker, about five feet up. No surprise. Brian loved getting high. No use trying to stop him. A homeboy from California, he brought his addiction with him.

"What the hell are you doing?" I said in a low voice.

"Wanna smoke a bowl of dew?" Brian, cupping both hands tightly over the glow of the smoke, raised his eyebrows. He never took much of anything seriously. This guy was the most unusual soldier ever. He was white but wanted to be Mexican, a Chicano. Raised in a barrio in East Los Angeles, he loved his new suntan, compliments of the tropical sun. He was skinny, always happy, balding, with a pock-marked face.

"You know I don't, man, and my patrol's not done yet. Who's up next on guard?" I asked.

"I don't know but they'll change places with me." He paused and added, "You're my best buddy, Sandy."

For some reason it was hard not to like the guy. "I'm crossing the road, see you later. I'll bring you some mud from the river, so your bald head won't shine in the moonlight."

"Hey, that's cool, man. I'll put some on my face. War paint."

"Okay, good."

"Hey, be careful man. I really mean it."

"Don't worry about me." I put my helmet back on.

★ ★ ★

ON THE THIRD CROSSING, I DEVISED A NEW PLAN. I WOULD take different directions this time. With grenades in my bag, I set out in the moonlight. First stop, I knelt. Dropped two grenades. *Whomp! Whomp!* The bag was noticeably lighter now.

Just a little way farther.

I dropped two more grenades and looked around.

Not a sound except for the exploding grenades. *Whomp!* *Whomp!* Very little disturbance in the water. I wondered whether the explosions killed any fish. Nothing appeared on the water. I checked my watch in the moonlight... 3:30 a.m. I sighed deeply and walked back to the bunkers.

Nesmith and Sergeant Stauder greeted me at the tower bunker.

"Hey, river rat!" Nesmith said.

I caught a different smell this time. *Hot chocolate.* "Well, you guys are really livin' it up in here. You got any extra?"

"Anything for the river guard." Stauder poured some of the drink from an old pot into a canteen cup. "Don't burn yourself."

I sipped. It tasted like the best I'd ever had. "This is the good stuff. Ya got any cookies?"

Nesmith held out what was called a silver cookie, the kind distributed in C Rations. Wrapped in foil and made from dry wheat and tropical chocolate, it was an insult to the word *cookie.*

"I'd rather eat the C Ration box. Thanks, anyway," I said.

After some time staring at the bottom of my cup, I lit a Marlboro. Two puffs. Then three. Then time to get back to the mission.

"You want more cocoa?" Nesmith smiled.

"No, I gotta get this thing over with."

After a quick visit to our outdoor latrine, I moved toward the water. Everything I could see glistened with moisture. Time to wrap this up before a blinding rain hits.

I dropped a grenade into the water, then immediately heard a chopper. Engine louder.

Louder!

A flash brighter than the sun hit me. A damn spotlight shone as the bird began circling the bridge, its eyes on me. *Sonofabitch!* I knelt. The trench gun lay flat on the bridge. *"Don't shoot me you bastards!"*

This had happened before at night in the field. Chopper crews shone a light on anything that looked suspicious.

I prayed now. If I heard the bird's M-60, I'd take my chances in the water under the bridge.

My heart pounded and leapt into my throat. One! Two! One! Two! One! Two! *How much longer? How much longer?*

The light blinked out.

The chopper flew off and I realized I'd been holding my breath all this time. I exhaled slowly.

The next sound to assault me was the rain, rain, rain, splashing everywhere, taking over. I stood up, then trudged back to safety. In one minute, everything was soaked. The land appeared different now; the thick air revived. Strange that it felt so good. Better than good, actually. Thank God.

And with that, my night patrol ended.

After I squared away my gear, I found my corner inside our bunker. I thought about home. I'd see my family again, go fishing, go to the movies, hang out, and maybe go to college. There'd be lots of girls at college. Fatigue quickly overwhelmed me.

As I dozed off, I wondered about the future. I dreamed of dry socks, glazed donuts, broiled steak, and then standing before a giant clock on a weathered red brick wall.

★ ★ ★

IN SIX WEEKS, TONTO WOULD LEAVE FOR CHICAGO TO BE with his family as the only surviving son after his brother was killed, along with 20 others, when a fire started from exploding ordinance aboard the Aircraft Carrier U.S.S. Forestall.

Brian would somehow survive a night ambush. With his chest and stomach filled with shrapnel from a booby trap, he went to a hospital in Japan, then home to Wilmington, California.

And me? I would be running for cover behind sandbags while 122-millimeter rockets rained down on Chu Lai Air Base while my company was there on a stand down.

That's when the name for our gang struck me.

Call this platoon the *Trench Guns*.

BOOMER'S LAMENT

"BOOMERS", THOSE BORN BETWEEN 1947 AND 1963, ARE subject to certain ailments that come with age such as dementia, which we prefer to call forgetfulness or absentmindedness or CRS (Can't Remember Stuff). In any case, if you can walk straight to where you parked your car after spending an hour in Home Depot, I admire your mental potency.

Additionally, as we age some people lose a degree of hearing and vision, or we begin to suffer joint pain and stiffness.

Recently a friend of mine, "Albert", made an appointment to see his doctor for shoulder pain and joint stiffness. Albert was prescribed medication to alleviate the condition, and sent to physical therapy. He understood that the pills should be taken with food.

On arriving home, he read over *The Patient Information Flyer*. The Flyer stated: *Your doctor has prescribed this medication for you because the benefits of it outweigh any negative effects.*

Be aware that this medication may cause the following side effects:

Nausea, gas, diarrhea, indigestion, headache, bloating, stomach cramps, dizziness, light-headedness, blurred vision, depression, ringing in the ears, or projectile vomiting of a substance that resembles coffee grounds. If you get diarrhea, do not take any medicine for this ailment before seeing your doctor. Also, please note that some forms of diarrhea are contagious. Be sure to take appropriate precautions.

You may appear cross-eyed at times or develop excessive ear wax.

You may experience blood in your stool, a sore throat, fatigue, and swelling of the feet or ankles.

May cause Stigmata in Catholics.

If you develop difficulty breathing, swallowing, swelling of your nose, thumbs or ears, stop taking this medication. If you begin doing bad impressions of actor Jack Nicholson, call your doctor immediately.

This medication may also cause continued sneezing, buck teeth, or barber's itch. Do not take this medication if you live in a Mountain Time Zone, or if you raise hamsters, or tend an ant farm.

Resist the temptation to dress like an Argentine Gaucho for one hour after taking this medication.

Women should not sing tunes from The Marriage of Figaro while taking this medication.

Eat only with your fingers, and do not try to smell anything. Ask your spouse or roommate or best friend to do this for you.

Do not answer phone calls with your hands.

You might also begin yodeling in your sleep.

You may think you are hearing messages from extra-terrestrials in the Romulan Galaxy. Ignore these messages. They are actually from the Planet Hygrotron, in Ptahh Galaxy.

This medication has been shown to cause pregnancy in women. If you think you are becoming pregnant, ask your doctor about wearing a chastity belt.

May cause x-ray vision. Alcohol will intensify this effect.

You may take this medication with Yak milk or fried Polish sausage.

Do not operate a stapler or light switch.

While taking this medication you may feel hungry just before having a meal. You may also feel tired and sleepy when first waking in the morning.

If you begin to feel nervous or anxious while taking this medication, remember: you must relax!

Keep this leaflet handy. You may need to read it again.

Finally, studies have shown that this medication has been known to cause joint pain and stiffness.

After reading the Flyer, Albert grabbed a beer from the fridge, popped open the pill bottle, then took his medication.

That night, the neighborhood dogs howled as Albert yodeled in bed.

TEMPRANO

PETER NOWAK SPIES WHAT LOOKS LIKE A BLACK AND white in the lane behind him. Grateful that he is carrying nothing more than a large amount of cash, he lights a cigarette. All the weed has been delivered to its new owner, ready for distribution. He slows, then turns his old rusted truck into a parking lot and stops in front of double glass doors marked *Waterman Convalescent.*

Stepping inside, he is greeted by a balding man wearing glasses and dressed in a white shirt. Pete steps up to the desk.

"It's me, right on time!" Pete hands the man a thick stuffed envelope.

The man takes the envelope, looks inside. "How much?"

"Well, $1900.00 today. That will cover the bill for two months, right?"

"You are correct sir!" The man smiles.

Pete leans forward. "Can I see her?"

"Well Pete, your little sister is in physical therapy right now and it takes a while for the attendants to do a good job." The man begins writing a receipt. "With the right treatment, she will be able to walk with braces."

"Okay, then. Please tell her I was here, okay?" Pete stops. He realizes no one will be able to *tell* his sister anything. The attendants at Waterman will use sign language. He hopes the therapy will help Amy overcome the conditions she was born with.

Pete has been home from the army and Vietnam for a year. Jobs were scarce with so many young men entering the job market. Every application he submitted was turned down or ignored. Through some friends in junior college, he learned that he could earn money delivering "product" to others for distribution. He finds the work easy and satisfying. It pays for his sister's care. He gives money to his mother and keeps what's left. His father left long ago.

Driving to his apartment, Pete thinks about his girlfriend Candy. Cute, petite, short blond hair, she likes Pete and wants to marry him. They met in high school. The two graduated in 1967, then he joined the army. Everyone but Pete thought it was a senseless thing to do. He reasoned that all his friends were going. The other reason was that he wanted adventure in life and the recruiter, a handsome, muscular sergeant in an impressive green uniform said, "it's a *steady paycheck.*"

Arriving at the apartment, he sees Candy's car parked outside. Approaching his door, he hears The Steve Miller Band playing *The Joker.* He finds Candy and her brother Norm inside.

Norm puts his beer down. "Hi, Pete, where ya bin?"

"Working. I stopped by the home to see Amy and pay a bill."

"That's good, Pete." Norm steps to open the refrigerator. "Ya wanna brew?"

Candy comes in from the kitchen. She grabs Pete. A long embrace and kiss. "You don't know how glad I am to see you.

The TV news said some marijuana was confiscated by San Diego police. Some people were arrested."

Ignoring her comment, Pete says, "I had a nice payday." He smiles as he removes his leather hand-tooled wallet. "Let's go out for lunch." Norm grabs his coat.

Pete is last, almost out the door as the phone rings. He picks up. "Hello, this is Pete." During a short conversation, Pete frowns. "Yeah, I get it, no problem." He hangs up.

During their restaurant meal, Candy puts down her fork. "Who called you, Pete? Was it your mom?" She smiles, then sips her iced tea. "We went grocery shopping yesterday, she's glad that Amy is making progress."

"It was nothing." Pete looks at his hamburger. "Just business." Putting ketchup on his french fries, he says, "I may be making an investment."

Candy leans forward and asks, "Like what? What are you gonna do?"

Pete rubs the back of his neck. "Well, I got the word from San Diego that with a bigger car, maybe a van, I could carry larger loads." He breathes deeply while drawing circles on his plate with a fry and ketchup. "I don't have much of a choice, you guys." Candy sighs.

The three go to a local auto dealer where Pete surveys the inventory. After discussion with a salesman, Pete hands over cash for a down payment. They made a deal on a new 1974 Econoline van, dark green, with all the extras.

Pulling out of the lot, Norm asks, "How much was the van, total?"

Pete looks at him. "You don't want to know." The van accelerates with Pete's smooth press on the gas pedal.

"If you ever need extra money to help pay for it, they're hiring down at the yard," Norm says.

Pete turns toward Norm. "Hey man, I'm not into hard labor," He laughs.

* * *

A FEW DAYS LATER, PETE DECIDES TO MAKE SOME improvements to his new wagon. First, a sound system, then a refrigerator, and finally a comfortable bed. He invites Candy to go with him to a hardware store to pick out some wood paneling for the van walls. The two look at what is available. Pete likes a dark walnut, but Candy prefers a much lighter birch color. She tells Pete they can both really look forward to good times with the van. Birch panel is loaded into the van. Later that evening Pete counts the stacks of money he has in his safe. He carefully locks it, has a beer, then goes to bed.

The next day, some of Pete's friends show up to admire his new van. After a short while, he asks them to leave. Later that evening, Pete gets word, by phone, that some product will arrive from San Diego. He has been preparing for a large shipment. The load will be going to a student at Colorado State for sale and distribution. Pete looks forward to checking the performance and comfort of the van.

Norm gets a call from Pete who explains that the two should meet at Norm's house the next morning.

After a night's sleep, some coffee and eggs, Pete drives to Norm's place—a half-acre lot where Norm lives in an old mobile home. A metal outbuilding sits in a field near some dry pine trees. Norm welcomes Pete, then swings open a heavy door. Candy has shown up with her brother.

Pete and Norm work with power tools to cut the paneling to size. Wood studs are cut and used with metal braces to fashion a walled van interior. The space between the wood and van body is hollow. The walls can easily be spread open with a small, flat pry bar. On completion, Pete asks to use Norm's telephone inside the house. Five minutes later, Pete returns.

"Need to get going. I'll be working for the next few days. Gotta pay bills, ya know." He smiles as he looks at the work done on the van. "This is a real professional job, Norm."

Norm puts down his beer. "What's coming in?"

"Just some weed. It's a short trip."

Candy steps up. "How long are you going to be doing this?"

"Just four or five days. No biggie."

Candy, raising her voice, says, "No, I mean how long can you keep taking chances like this?" She points at the van.

Surprised, Pete says, "This one pays really good." He touches her shoulders. "When I get back, we can talk."

Candy crosses her arms as she looks down. "Yeah, we can talk." She walks toward the house, shaking her head.

Pete leaves to meet couriers from San Diego at a secluded spot off the highway in the San Bernardino mountains. Twelve kilos are loaded into the van walls under the shade of a few pine trees. He thanks the couriers and begins his trip to Fort Collins. He will stop one night in Albuquerque, stay with an acquaintance, then move on to Colorado.

The scenery through Arizona is amazing. Pete passes by Saguaro Cactus at least eight feet tall. Light green, a tall center trunk, with four to five spines the size of baseball bats reaching upward from the trunk. Occasional mustard seed bushes, small yellow flowers waving, follow some stretches of desert highway. A pair of hawks fly over, seen from an angle high up in front of the van. *This is a beautiful ride to the top of the world!*

An hour passes, then two. Soon this mission will be over and he can continue to pay for his sister's care and help support his mom. He can also feed the growing stash in his safe. Reaching the state line, he sees a roadside greeting: *Welcome To New Mexico—Land of Enchantment.* Perfect. It won't be long before he hits Albuquerque, then north to unload the shipment.

After some time, the land is almost totally flat, with but a few tall dry bushes, and an occasional roadside green tree. He rarely smokes but decides to light a cigarette.

Along the lonely highway, Pete marvels at how easy the trip has been. He sees a rock formation while rounding a curve. It appears as a huge animal waiting to cross the road, its mouth partly open. Later, a metal sign wearing bullet holes: *Temprano Population 24. That's my age*, Pete thinks. He has been down this road before but does not recall ever seeing the sign. Temprano?

Finishing his cigarette, he spies what looks like a patrol car in his side view mirror. *Where did that come from?* As the two vehicles move along, the car behind closes distance. Pete confirms that it is a black and white, a red, bubble-shaped light protruding from its roof. *Son of a bitch!* Pete cringes as he hopes the car will change lanes and pass him.

No such luck. A final flash of red light and siren squawk causes Pete to pull over. Pete can play it cool, no problem. Just a trip to New Mexico to visit some student friends.

The deputy leaves his car and approaches the van. Tall, with a thick dark mustache. A western hero in a Stetson.

Pete rolls down his window. "What's up, officer?"

"I stopped you because you were speeding." The deputy looks at the dashboard, then back at Pete. "Got your license and registration? This won't take long." The deputy extends a weathered hand, a silver star on his ring finger.

Pete takes the registration from the glove box. He hands it over to the deputy with his driver's license. He knows he wasn't speeding, but it's always better not to argue.

"Be right back son." The deputy steps back to his car.

Pete is sweating now, partly from the heat, mostly from nervousness. After what seems like an hour, the deputy returns to Pete's window.

The deputy starts to hand the license back as he eyeballs the inside of the van. He sees an alligator clip attached to the driver's side visor. "Very nice van. Is it new?" Before Pete can answer, the deputy wants to know more. "What's this?"

Pete, with difficulty, responds, "It's just a clip to hold a map up there."

"Please carefully step out of the van, son. Keep your hands in plain sight at all times." The deputy removes handcuffs from his belt. "Don't get jumpy, just relax."

"What's goin' on?"

"Don't argue, son. Get out of the van." Pete steps out. He is cuffed. "This is for my safety and yours. Relax. We just gotta have a look inside your van."

Pete is doing his best to remain calm. "What do you mean? Why?"

"Well, that clip on your visor can be used to smoke the last of a marijuana cigarette." The deputy, holding the tips of his thumb and index finger together, then to his lips, he pretends to puff an imaginary smoke. "That's drug paraphernalia son—a roach clip."

Ridiculous, Pete thinks. "Oh, I don't know anything about that stuff." Nothing will be found. Everything is secure in the van.

The deputy opens the van rear doors. He looks inside, then sniffs a wall while tapping it with his flashlight. Humming a deep tune, he removes a buck knife from his belt, he cuts then pries open part of the paneling. "What's in here?" He shines his flashlight inside the open wall.

Pete, barely controlling his breathing, says, "I don't know. Insulation or something."

The buck knife opens more of the van wall. "I think you got a whole van load of pot in here, son!" The deputy walks Pete over to the black and white. After the two are seated inside, the deputy, says, "You are now under arrest. We are gonna take a little ride." The car's back wheels kick up dirt as it leaves the road shoulder.

The car makes a trip off the main highway onto a bumpy dirt road. After a while, nearing what looks like a town, Pete sees some donkeys walking on the road. "What are those? Are they from a ranch?"

"They're wild, left over from the old copper mine days." The deputy leans on the horn. The animals barely pick up their pace.

Pete is delivered to a small weathered shack of a police station. The town is so small it looks like an old western movie set. As he is taken from the car, a donkey looks his way. It snorts, then moves on. *Is this for real?*

Pete is taken inside where a fat man wearing dirty, oil-stained overalls sits behind a desk. He asks the deputy what he has. The deputy replies. The fat man stands, salutes, then says he will have the van towed to the shop.

The deputy removes the handcuffs, then looks Pete in the eye. "Mr. Nowak, you are a special case." He tips his hat back, then rubs his eyes. "With your cooperation, we can take care of this matter with a minimum of trouble for all of us. Have you ever been arrested?"

"No. I never have." He clears his throat, then swallows hard. "What is your name, officer? Have I been charged? When will I get to see a lawyer?"

The deputy squints, then smiles. "Well, you gotta whole load of questions, don't you boy? Just be patient. Ya want some water?" The deputy steps over to a dust-covered water dispenser. He tips it forward to spill the last of the contents into a cracked coffee mug. "Here ya go, boy." Pete takes the cup, drinks, then gags.

Pete is placed back in the patrol car, then taken to a house on a rocky hill overlooking the town. There, he is ushered into a large room resembling a library—the walls adorned with Native American artifacts along with swords and landscape portraits. He is handcuffed again. The deputy pulls a heavy antique chair to the center of the room. Pete is told to sit. He wonders what is happening and how he got into this. The nameless deputy stands behind him.

After a few minutes, a thin gray-haired man enters the room and takes a seat at a massive wooden desk. The man speaks.

"Welcome to the town of Temprano, sir." The man coughs. "You are being charged with possession of drug paraphernalia and dangerous drugs. I am the judge here. Are you prepared to enter a plea? I assure you that whatever the sentence, it will be a fair one." Crooked yellow teeth shine with each word.

Pete stands up. "Don't I get a free lawyer and go to a real court? I don't understand any of this!"

The deputy drives a hammer fist into the side of Pete's head. "Don't be disrespectful, boy, or this can get a lot worse!" Pete gasps as he falls back into the chair.

Yellow Teeth finds a pipe on his desk. "Oh, such hostility." He stuffs the pipe and lights it. He puffs while he taps his fingers on the desk. "Take the prisoner back to a cell. We will convene again tomorrow." He leans back while admiring the artwork on his walls.

★ ★ ★

BACK AT THE STATION, PETE IS UNCUFFED AND PLACED, alone, in an unlocked cell. After an hour, a cheerful woman, heavy set, wearing thick glasses, brings him oatmeal and coffee for his dinner. She swings the cell door open, then enters.

"Here we ahhh-are! At least the coffee is hot." She carefully places the meal on the cot against the cell wall. "Stay well. The judge will be here in the morning. Maybe you can plea a deal or something, it's not so bad." She smiles. "You are such a nice-looking boy."

"Have others done the same? About the plea, I mean." Pete rubs his hands together. "Is there a real court here in town, with a lawyer to defend me?"

"Oh, I don't know. The court may talk about that tomorrow." She cocks her head. "Others have stayed here in the cell. I try to keep it clean. God knows we've asked the state for more money." Her sing-song voice dripped with honey. She turns away. "The doors are not locked. We treat inmates here with respect. But please don't try to leave. If the town folk see someone wandering at night, they might shoot first, you know. Let me know if you need an extra blanket. Good night, honey." She steps out.

"Wait. How will I find you? I'd have to leave the cell!"

This must be a dream. Pete wonders again how this all started. The oatmeal smells like a week's worth of dirty laundry. Drained mentally and emotionally, he drinks the coffee. He recalls how he was encouraged by Candy and his mom to learn a trade when he left the army. Why didn't he try doing that? He prays that he can escape with his life, then falls asleep on the dirty cot as mice cross the cell floor. That night he has a strange dream that he is being chased by donkeys.

* * *

THE NEXT MORNING PETE WAKES TO THE SOUND OF Cheery Lady. She offers him coffee and a stack of buttered toast sprinkled with cinnamon and sugar. "Here you go-ohh! I just love this kind of toast, don't you? I know *I* do!" Pete takes the meal from her. "The judge will be here soon. He's a nice man."

Pete runs his fingers through his curly dark hair. He thinks about offering a bribe but realizes that these people are crazy and would just add another charge. Trying to suppress fear, he wonders what these people will do with him. He starts laughing at the thought of throwing himself at the mercy of the court.

Yellow Teeth, the Deputy and the Cheery Lady enter and take places outside the cell. They park themselves in lawn chairs brought in by the fat man Pete saw earlier wearing the filthy overalls. He leans against a wall.

The deputy stands to speak. "All rise! Let the power of the State of New Mexico shine on this honorable hearing today. Court is now in session, the Honorable Hampton Foghorn presiding."

The judge eyes Pete. "This court is here to decide the fate of one Peter Nowak, a Californian, who has in violation of law brought illegal contraband into our state and with malice through the road to Temprano, a God-Fearing town." He clears his throat. "At this time, Mr. Nowak, you are allowed to address this court. What do you have to say for yourself." He leans slightly forward with a furrowed brow. "You are reminded to show respect."

Respect. *That's funny*, Pete thinks. *Okay, here goes.* Maybe appealing to their better nature, if they have one, will help. Maybe he can speak their language.

"Sir, your honor, I know I have done a terrible, horrible wrong." Tilting his head back, he takes a breath. "If I can, I would like the people of Temprano to know how sorry I am."

He puts his hand over his heart. Cherry Lady nods her head. "Truly sorry." Suddenly, real tears flow. "If possible, I would like to know what kind of plea I may be allowed, your honor. As I remember the honorable deputy told me that I was a special case, sir."

The judge snorts as he turns to the deputy. "Did you tell the defendant that?"

"Yes, I did, your honor."

Turning back to Pete, the judge points his finger at him and says, "All right then! Let us continue. I don't suppose you would mind giving up that nice Ford van, would you?" The judge leans forward again. "And Mr. Nowak, *I know* you would not think that you can keep all that dope stored in it."

"No, your honor. I will give up everything without question, sir." Pete clears his throat. "One thing your honor. The van is not paid for."

"Does it have air conditioning?"

"Yes, sir."

The judge rubs his chin, "All right, fine, *we* will pay it off. The lady here will take care of everything."

Cheery Lady writes a note, and hands it to the man in overalls. He smiles as he leaves.

"All right. This matter is concluded. Mr. Nowak. The Deputy here will give you the special case terms of your release. God Bless this honorable court! Dismissed!"

Everyone leaves, except the deputy, who takes Pete outside. He wonders, what does *release* mean? If he is going to be shot, he will fight with all he's got. His stomach churns and knots as he waits.

"Okay son, here's the deal. You say you were going to Albuquerque. Right?" The deputy places his hands on his hips. "We will give you a voucher to use for a bus ride from here to there. When you get there, you can do whatever the hell you want." He straightens his hat. "Don't think about telling anybody about our little town. You got connections in your line of work… well we got connections, too." The deputy puts a hand on Pete's shoulder. "I used to be FBI."

Pete winces. He doesn't know whether to believe it or not.

With voucher in hand, Pete is driven to a barren spot off the main highway a few miles out. Pete is suspicious but gets out of the car. The deputy explains, through an open window, that Pete should just stand next to a rotted, single fence post near the road. Wait there, and a bus will appear and stop for him. He laughs and tells Pete to bring another van next time he comes through.

As the patrol car turns around to leave, Pete picks up a tennis ball size rock. It takes a strong will to keep from throwing it.

Standing in the sun, Pete wonders if there really is a bus. An hour later, he sees it in the distance. As the bus approaches, the words "Greyhound" appear between the bumper and windshield. He holds up his voucher as the huge vehicle slows for him. Its arrival is marked by hissing air brakes. The doors open, and the driver and Pete stare at each other for a moment.

"Well, are you getting on?"

"Yeah, yeah, I'm just a little tired." Pete steps up and hands the voucher to the driver. "How long a ride to Albuquerque?"

"Bout two and a half hours. Take a seat"

On the way, feeling safe now, Pete can't help but think of himself as a total loser. He thought he had it all figured out. *Maybe that town was just a horrible dream.*

Making it to Albuquerque, Pete calls his friend to come and get him at the main bus station. The friend asks Pete where he has been, and what happened to him. The friend tells Pete that he really needs a shower. Pete simply brushes off all comments.

After a night in town, he borrows money to get back home. At the bus station, he buys some headache pills. *This is the only drug I want to have with me ever,* he thinks.

During the ride home, he wonders whether they are still hiring at the yard.

THE DRAFT

THE BUS WAS AS COLD AND DRAB AS AN ARMY BUS CAN BE...
a reflection of the Pacific Northwest weather itself: faded green
with alternating streaks of black and gray near the wheel wells...
unwashed tires... windows nearly frosted over from bouts with
the elements. Inside the vehicle, chatter from a load of troops
on the way from Fort Lewis, Washington to a nearby airport
for an all-expense paid trip to the Orient was the only warm
and friendly sound.

Nixon was in office. Gasoline was 34 cents a gallon.
Movie tickets cost $1.50, and someone killed Senator Robert
Kennedy. Near the base gate, the bus rattled to one more stop
in front of a white, two-story wooden barracks. The driver,
smelling of cigarette smoke, opened the door.

A small, goofy-looking kid dragged a duffel bag up the
steps. Breathing heavily, with a portable radio under his arm,
his complexion was like that of a cream puff. His green cap,
creased unevenly, covered half of one ear.

He was an easy target.

"Where did you get the hat... at the circus?" The troops
began having their fun.

"Hey, this is the army, not a kindergarten bus!" Laughter.

"He escaped from the zoo!" Roaring laughter.

The kid pulled his kit down the aisle and said in a low voice, "Yeah, well I seen better lookin' than you."

A Black trooper yelled, "Hey man, what's your bag? Turn on the radio so we can hear it!"

The kid sat and began fiddling with the radio. Next, the unexpected happened. Jerry Butler, an A-list soul singer of the time, came on singing, "*...only the strong survive, only the strong survive. Hey, you gotta be strong, you better hold on... hold on.*"

The timeworn bus pulled away and exited the base.

Silence.

★ ★ ★

ON ARRIVAL IN COUNTRY, CREAMPUFF SETTLED INTO HIS clerk's job in the brigade Tactical Operations Center, the "TOC", a wooden, heavily-sandbagged structure near the center of Landing Zone Dollar. He adapted to the daily teasing from other troops. Over time, it didn't matter to him. But it never stopped.

"Hey Creampuff, you look sick. Will ya be able to handle a typewriter today?"

"Get some sun on you, man!"

"Do somethin' 'bout those skinny arms."

"Better stay inside, the wind will blow you away!"

It was not unusual to find loose gear deposited on his cot at night when he needed to get to sleep. One time, someone poured water on his blanket. "Hey look, Creampuff wet the bed!"

One night, a siren blared over the company street. Viet Cong sappers had breached the wire. Their plan was apparently to run wild through the LZ tossing explosives at the small plywood barracks, vehicles, bunkers—anything that could be destroyed.

An armed guard outside the TOC jumped inside. Radio operators, along with Creampuff got down and huddled under wooden counters and chairs. Explosions outside along with sporadic gunfire filled the air.

A sudden yell. "*Nem no!*" —throw it!

A satchel charge flew into the bunker. It kicked up dust as it landed on the wood floor. Someone shined a flashlight on it. Collective gasps followed.

"Cover up!" someone shouted.

"With what?" screamed another. The concussion from the blast would be enough to kill everyone and they knew it. All six men froze.

Creampuff squinted at the unwelcome canvas bag. No one expected what happened next. He jumped up, grabbed the bag, then ran out into the dark.

One man, crying and muttering Hail Mary's, peered up from the dirt. It took a few seconds for the bunker crew to realize that Creampuff had disappeared. Then a huge explosion rattled the TOC and shook the earth.

★ ★ ★

BY MORNING, THE LZ WAS CLEAR. MEN CLEANED UP, securing the area, and tended to the wounded. Smoke hovered over the destruction. In an open area, at the end of the company street, a large swath had been cleared of dry grass by a blast from the night before. The guys from TOC gaped at the charred space while looking for Creampuff.

"I don't think he made it," someone said.

As they walked to the aid station, they were amazed to see what looked like Creampuff sitting outside on a wooden ammo crate. *It was him.* His face was red and covered in dirt. He stood up as the group approached him, and tilted his head. "Hi guys," he smiled, his voice weak. He looked so much older now.

The men gathered around him. "What happened, man?"

He began shaking, then silently pointed in the direction of the bare dirt blast area. The men stared at Creampuff with deep respect.

"I gotta write home," he said. Then he pulled his shoulders back and walked away.

"Hey wait! The medics should see you!" one man said.

Another replied, "Let him go, let him go... he's better than all of us."

ANYTHING BUT A DIRECT HIT

LINDA LANDERS SAT IN CRIMINAL COURT WITH HER *lawyer and waited for the jury to return. The only other times she had hired counsel occurred when she needed help with evictions or obtaining title to distressed properties. Today, she had hired the best defense.*

So, what was she doing here? She gazed at the huge gold crest on the wall behind the judge's bench, then her mind floated back to the evening when she stopped her car on the street...

★ ★ ★

TRAFFIC STOOD STILL ON THE SIDE STREET OFF THE boulevard. Linda Landers wanted to drive past a fourplex she was interested in purchasing near a commercial district. She smelled smoke and saw a fire engine blocking the street ahead. Red lights flashed in sync to the sound of a diesel engine. *Now what?* It was getting dark. She had hoped to see the fourplex in daylight.

Impatient at the delay, she stopped and opened the door of her sporty BMW while she set one foot on the street to survey the situation. As she peered from behind the open door, she saw two kids on the sidewalk.

Linda called out to them. "What happened?"

"Dan set fire to a big dumpster because there was no food in it!"

"Who?"

"Dumpster Dan!"

Linda sat back in her car, then turned around to avoid traffic. She knew about the so-called homeless in the city. There were more of these vagrants in town each day. Some businesses had posted "No Trespassing" signs in parking lots trying to keep the influx at bay. She recalled that the city had given up twenty square blocks to them downtown. The deal was that the bums, as she called them, could not block sidewalks with tents and furniture. *Unreal,* thought Linda.

The surrender happened even as rats and disease grew in that part of the city. Who was going to stop this? A friend told her that the rats were spreading plague, a disease from the dark ages.

Linda's M8 Coupe moved along gracefully, a reward to herself from the sale of one of her properties after her husband died. The two had enjoyed a good life together buying, selling, and rehabbing properties.

Three-bedroom, two-bath family homes were their best investment. Benny was a good man who took opportunities as they came. He'd been an insurance agent for over 20 years, and he knew the city well, having driven the streets to see clients. Benny then took Linda out to see homes on the verge of foreclosure. Loans and creative financing, one deal at a time, led to an accumulation of property and wealth.

Benny passed away in his sleep one night at home, the victim of an undiagnosed heart condition. Linda remembered that he would often say, before downing a shot of Bushmills, that, "the best deals are yet to come... the *lack* of money is the root of all evil." His death left her in shock for weeks until her friend Mark Stevens, the family real estate broker, reminded her that she had properties to manage, and most importantly rents to collect and deposit.

The visit to the fourplex would wait until tomorrow. Mark would be there, his fast-talking cheery disposition always made Linda smile, even if she was not ready to deal.

As she arrived home, she used the remote control to open the garage door, and she shut down the car's 6-cylinder turbo-charged engine. Since she lived alone, she checked her purse for her .38 revolver and pepper spray. As she stepped into her huge split-level home, she turned on the lights. Something occurred to her. If only Benny was here to see this. So much passive income, the car, the new home, places she has been. Money. And not a care in the world.

★ ★ ★

THE NEXT MORNING DURING BREAKFAST, LINDA READ the city section of her newspaper. Rent control was the latest issue. The state legislature wanted to cap rent increases at 2% per year. Linda's husband taught her that at least 4% plus inflation should be the rule. The cost of housing continued to increase. A city council member wanted to budget for homeless services.

While Benny was alive, Linda and her daughter, Amy, would volunteer to serve meals at a shelter. Amy, young and idealistic, coaxed Linda to come out to help in the community. After a few visits to lend a hand, Linda saw that many people who showed up looked like they had not missed any meals for some time. Most of the men were unwashed, even though there were facilities for them to clean up. Every man who came for a meal appeared able-bodied.

Linda thought they should try to earn their way somewhere instead of standing on the corner with a cardboard sign that read, "Please Help, Need Food." Most of this money went to booze and drugs, Linda was sure of it. She became disgusted with the shelter and "clients" when Amy began giving money and urged her mother to do the same.

Linda was sure that Amy's efforts could be put to better use elsewhere. If people needed a place to live, she would provide it and tenants would pay for it.

Amy, disappointed, told her mother that she would eventually see that the poor were no different from the rest. After studying drama for a time in junior college, Amy moved north to take a job in Portland with a community theater group. *What a useless profession that is*, she thought.

As Linda sipped her coffee, her cell rang. The screen displayed the name "Mark". He had a talent for bringing properties to Linda at below market prices. Linda was grateful for that. She inhaled deeply as she stood. A silky robe hung from her thin frame, her bright blue eyes and clear complexion added to her mature attractiveness.

"Hello Mark, what's happening today? What's on the menu?"

"Are you ready for the sweetest deal on that fourplex we talked about earlier? We can have a look at the outside today and set up an interior inspection later, subject to owners' agreement and notice to the tenants."

"I might be able to fit it into my schedule."

"Well, with it being occupied and no evictions pending, you may want to jump on this one." Mark knew Linda played hard to get. His upbeat voice sounded like that of a young TV game show host. "Let's meet there at around ten. I can get a few pictures and see whether it's worth... what the seller might want."

"Then get it for less!" Linda said.

"Okay, then. You know where it is. I'll see you there at ten."

Linda prepared to see the property. She already knew its worth. After running numbers on tax benefits such as mortgage interest, property tax, insurance, operating expenses, depreciation and repairs, Linda believed that she was looking at an excellent deal. If the price was right.

After her shower, she chose a pair of faded jeans, worn tennis shoes and a bland color top as her outfit—the least threatening—a not so wealthy image she wanted to present. Most tenants must be treated with kid gloves. Linda made it clear that people should not consider her projected good nature as weakness on her part.

Her home, with a floor to ceiling fireplace, created a rustic yet ornate image in the main room. She made her way down to the 3-car garage and chose her old '96 Lincoln V-8 for her drive. *The last of the muscle cars*, she called it. The last thing Linda wanted anyone to see today was a newer, shiny, expensive sports car.

As she drove through town, Linda considered the work it would take to get a new property up to her standards. Painting would be the biggest expense.

Linda pulled up past the fourplex to park in front of a house down the block. She strolled along the street. A good way to determine the quality of a neighborhood was to observe whether there were toys scattered in front of a house, or whether young men milled about smoking or drinking, and whether the landscaping was acceptable.

As she passed in front of the property, she noticed an alley running alongside it. Across from the alley stood rear walls of small businesses, their fronts facing a four-lane boulevard. A chain link fence, partly beaten down, ran next to the alley separating the businesses from the fourplex. Some trash was scattered about.

The wood frame two-story appeared to be in "okay" shape from the outside. It desperately needed paint. Linda was about to step onto the wooden wraparound porch to get a better look, but hesitated.

She peered to the street as Mark pulled up in his four-door Ford truck. Dressed in the usual expensive slacks and golf shirt, he jumped from the vehicle.

He waved to Linda as he walked toward her, and moving his sunglasses to just above his forehead, he said, "Linda, how are you dear? Do you need a hug?" He took her hand in both of his, then released it and wrapped his arms around her.

"Well! It's good to see you." Linda hugged back, gently, careful to refrain from becoming aroused by the feel and smell of such a young handsome man.

"You're looking good! Ready to take some of the cold cash from the freezer to expand your portfolio?"

"Let's look around. I see the place needs some paint and the alley probably has vagrants traveling through at all hours. And... we'll need a roof inspection before any closing, if I buy it at all."

Mark took the mention of a professional inspection as a signal that Linda was interested. He continued. "Sure, let's walk around the place. The owner has informed the tenants that he was going to sell and that we would be here to look around. We can make an offer contingent on an inside inspection."

As the two walked to the porch, they scared a couple of cats away from an old couch sitting there. Linda hated cats but said nothing.

Mark smiled. "All four apartments are occupied with no evictions pending. These tenants are all employed long term. That's what I got from the owner."

Linda turned to face Mark. "So, what is he collecting in rents? What's the reason for selling?"

"Landlord is collecting $950.00 per month on each unit."

Linda frowned. "Oh man, is that all? These are two-bedroom units, right?"

"Yes, so there is some room for a rent increase, absolutely."

She surveyed the fourplex and the buildings across the street. "These should be going for eleven fifty to twelve—even in this neighborhood. Does he pay for trash pickup?"

"Yes, it helps to keep the place looking good. Some properties have weeds in the yard. This place has green grass in front. A little water and fertilizer, and some new bushes will polish it up even more."

Linda glanced at the yard. "Well, it looks clean enough, like the owner has trained his tenants. Let's look around back."

The two walked around the building. Occasionally, they checked the eaves for wood rot or termite damage. "This backyard is huge," Linda said. "You could build another place back here."

"Good thinking, Linda. Just put in for the permits, muster some cash and you're off to the races. Double your income and reduce tax liabilities!"

She placed her hand on his arm, stopping him. "Why is the place for sale?"

Mark shrugged. "The guy is a widower, getting older with no children living in the state. He hardly ever hears from them unless they want money. He's tired of living in California." Mark rubbed his hands together. "He plans to leave the state. 'First stop is Las Vegas,' he said." Mark laughed. "He talked of going to Costa Rica. He's been there before when he was in the navy stationed in the Panama Canal Zone."

"Well how much does he want?"

"That's the good news. The place can be yours for just… drum roll, $380,00.00. That's $95,000 per unit!"

Linda lifted her eyes to the upper floor. She paused, expressionless. "Take me to lunch so we can talk about it some more."

"You got it, Linda."

The two returned to the sidewalk. A man pushing a shopping cart full of plastic bottles, aluminum cans and rags shuffled through the alley in the direction of Mark's truck. Though the day was heating up, the man wore a long, dirty overcoat. His shoes should have been discarded long ago. He had a limp. His hair and beard were shaggy, and the color? Battleship gray. This was problematic.

"You didn't tell me about *castaways* in the area," Linda said, using the nicest word she could think of.

"Hey Linda, it's a fact of life. This guy cleans up around here. He gathers the cans and plastic to sell."

"Making an honest living, I suppose." Still, Linda had to admit that the likes of these lost souls appeared to be growing.

At times, she wished she had the courage to approach one who didn't seem demented, to ask, "How the hell did you get this way?"

"Where do we go for lunch, Linda?'

"Okay, how about that Italian place down the boulevard? What's the name?"

"You're thinking of Arianna's Garden. Let's meet there. We can beat the lunch rush; it's a great place."

The two drove separately to Arianna's, Mark, thinking about the potential deal and commission. Linda wondered, *what will it cost? What can I collect in rents? What can I sell it for in five years? What is the market doing?*

She'd want $5,000.00 in total rent, per month, to make it worthwhile. Oh, the money that she would make!

After arriving at Arianna's, Mark and Linda entered to the smell of fresh bread from the oven. "This place has the best lasagna, and the best bread rolls to go with any dish served," Mark said, practically salivating.

A waitress greeted them. She showed them to a table picked by Mark. Linda checked the wine list, then got right to the point. "What kind of concessions do you think we can get from the seller?"

"Well, with the market being what it is for multi-family housing, the seller's mood, location, and time of year, I figure no more than 5%, with each party paying their own costs 50-50."

"So, we're looking at $360,000... maybe."

"A 5% discount is a good deal, Linda. You can shine the place up and sell in six or seven years, then move up to a six or eightplex, multiple apartments. That's where some real money can be made." Mark's voice, smile and good looks eased any concern Linda had.

She thought about the property for a moment as the waitress came to take their orders. She ordered a chicken caesar salad and wine... Mark, a meatball sandwich with beer.

Linda sipped her drink. "There's the potential for adding another multi-family in the back, too... if the local bums don't overrun the place."

"Linda, the city is looking at ways to control stuff like that through code enforcement. The city owns the alley as far as I know, and they have responsibility for it." Mark put his hands together. "There's no graffiti on the back walls or back of the businesses, right?"

During their discussion, the waitress brought lunch with a serving of soft, square, puffy rolls—a tasty restaurant specialty. Linda immediately helped herself. Mark took a bite of his sandwich.

"I'll make an offer of $360,000, and I will pay half the seller's costs. Does that make your lunch taste better?" She knew that getting a loan, with Mark's help, would not be a problem. She was aware of the advantages of using OPM—other people's money. "I can give my man Whitney a call about some work I may have for him."

Mark smiled like a man whose horse won the race. He had a duty to present any offer, even the "low ball" Linda was pitching.

Whitney's crew currently worked a job on the other side of town next to the freeway. They had been pulling up old carpet from one of Linda's properties. The tenants left the place with minimal wear and tear. The interior would need to be painted—a simple task—and the crew had paint and all the necessary equipment to do the work, including a quality paint sprayer. A four-bedroom, two bath with a large, fenced front and backyard and fireplace would bring increased rent of at least $2700.00 per month. Linda was counting on it.

One night, several months ago, thieves stole tools and materials from the site. Whitney asked Linda for an increase in the job cost, but she was not agreeable. Instead, she told Whitney to have someone stay in the empty house overnight to guard it. She said the tools should have been insured and if not, well, that wasn't her problem. This attitude left Whitney disappointed. Always the profit motive.

* * *

THE NEXT DAY, MARK ROSE EARLY WITH PLANS TO CALL the seller of the fourplex. After arriving at his office, he checked his notes and practiced the pitch he would present to Marty before calling. He hit the speed dial on his phone.

"Hello?" The rasp of Marty's voice nearly drove Mark's ear away.

"Mr. Martin, this is Mark Stevens. How's your morning going?"

"So far, so good. What's going on with the property? Any solid buyer yet?"

"Great news! We have an offer. Subject to interior inspection, of course." Mark took a deep breath. He waited for Marty's response.

"Hmm... how much? They're not tryin' to lowball me, are they Mark?"

"It's $360,000, with the buyer paying half the costs of escrow. This will put more money in your pocket at closing, Marty. You'll be free from responsibility and headaches of land lording for good!" Mark stared at his computer screen. "You can calendar travel dates or find yourself a low-cost place to live out of state if you want. What do you think?"

"Lemme get myself a drink and I'll call you back." Marty's tone was hard to read. He took the cap off a half pint of whiskey, then dribbled some into his coffee mug.

"Ohhhh-kay Marty, please don't take too long. We don't want this buyer to get away."

"I'll call back today. I just need to look into my bank account and social security income ledger, okay Mark?"

"Fine Marty, talk soon!" As he placed the phone in its cradle, Mark's confidence that he could make a deal on this one grew. He would get the full 6% commission, as he was both the seller's and buyer's agent. He remembered when he started out in the business that the Real Estate Board cautioned all new agents not to think of the unwritten agreement between agents to charge the 6% as price fixing. Woe unto anyone who ever dared to think of or call it that. But that is what it was: price fixing... maintaining commissions at a certain level by all competing offices and agents.

Mark had owned rental properties. He decided to quit being a landlord after realizing that one can never wake up one morning and say to themselves, I am no longer a landlord charged with the responsibilities of caring for people who lack the smarts to buy their own place, or any smarts, and who might call at midnight to complain that a light bulb had burned out. These thoughts entertained him as he waited for Marty's return call.

Without a warning, he was interrupted by the melodic ring of the phone. Marty was on the line to accept the offer contingent on an interior inspection of the property. The news was joy to Mark's ears. After the conversation, he prepared to call Linda with the good news and discuss a time to show her the inside.

Once the parties had agreed on an inspection date, Marty called each tenant to tell them that he would be selling the fourplex to a new, responsible and dependable owner, and that all tenants would remain in the building. Everything would be the same as before.

As the date approached, Mark and Linda prepared by putting on their best game faces. The idea was to be friendly, agreeable, outgoing, and receptive during inspection. All tenants had been notified.

The day before inspection, Linda drove by the fourplex to see if any trash or junk near the property had appeared. Then, more vagrants gathered near the alley. She wished that she could wave a magic wand to make them disappear. The hard-nosed part of her even contemplated hiring someone to deal with them in some... *alternative* way. But that would lead to other problems.

* * *

THE NEXT DAY, MARK, MARTY, AND LINDA MET AT THE property. After a brief meet and greet, Marty left as Mark and Linda approached the first downstairs apartment. Marty had briefed them both earlier about what to expect from the tenants.

Joseph West was a tall muscular Black man. He shared the apartment with his ten-year-old son. He held two jobs: one as a truck driver, and a second as a fry cook. That way, he provided what his son needed. The boy, Gabe, went to a private school. Joe was able to send his son to play basketball and learn karate, the latter to protect himself from bullies. Gabe learned to live Christian ideals from his dad.

Joe's wife had died from cancer three years after Gabe was born. He saved his money so that he and Gabe could move to a nicer place. They learned, much to Linda's interest, that he kept a watchful eye on homeless people in the area.

Mark knocked on Joe's door. The man answered, greeting his visitors with a broad smile. "Hello, are you the new landlords?"

"I'm the real estate agent," said Mark, "this is Linda Landers. She's thinking of buying the fourplex".

Joe extended his hand to Linda then asked them to come in.

"Okay, this is it. Have a look around, Linda," said Mark.

Joe stood back, then said, "It's comfortable here. We do our best to take care of the place."

"Well, that's good," Linda said, "we appreciate tenants who care." Mark and Linda took a quick look around, stopping to check under the sinks in the kitchen and bathroom for any leaks or potential problems. "You live here with your son, correct?"

"Yes, he's a good boy."

"Okay, Mr. West. If I take over as landlord, I have a great handyman who can take care of any problems in your place... just let us know."

"Call me Joe, ma'am. I do have a question: do you think the rent will go up if you take over?"

Linda knew the tenants might ask about that. "Well, that's a possibility." Linda knew she did not have to disclose her finances to renters. "If it increases, it won't be any higher than the rate of inflation. We can go over it later." Linda saw cash rolling in. Joe sighed and nodded in agreement.

Mark and Linda went next door to visit two more tenants: Chris and Kirby were two young men who became friends while both served in the Navy. The two moved in together after their service time was up. They registered at community college, taking courses in teaching and nursing.

Chris, hearing a knock, opened the door. "Hey guys, come in. I'm Chris."

Mark introduced himself and Linda. "Hey Chris, we're here to look at the inside. Linda is a potential buyer."

"Well, this is a nice place, we don't have any complaints. We always have hot water, and the air conditioning is good. Kirby's at school."

The place was very well kept. Kitchen counters were clear, except for the coffee maker, toaster and microwave. The sink was empty. The floors were swept. At one point, Linda, careful to make sure no one was looking, ran her finger over a windowsill—not a hint of dust.

Chris, while seated reading a book and having coffee, asked whether the inspectors needed to talk to Kirby.

"No, it's not necessary," replied Linda. "We had a good look, and we'll be going."

Chris stood to open the door. "Okay, let us know if you need anything. Just call, okay?"

"Yes, thanks. Good day, and say hello to Kirby."

Mark and Linda stepped outdoors. "Did you see how clean the place was, Linda?"

"Yes, almost too clean." Linda, wary of tenants, wondered if they might be hiding something.

Two more units remained to inspect. At the next apartment, Mark and Linda met "Oakie" as he was called. He lived on Social Security and vodka, and was content to live alone with his "cop memories." He met Mark and Linda at the door, showed them in, then sat at his computer.

Oakie was a brawny fellow with a thick Brooklyn accent. His place was sparse, lacking a lot of furniture, but it held the bare necessities: fridge, toaster, coffee maker, radio, TV, and a table with two maple wood chairs. An antique filing cabinet stood in a corner, and artificial plants sat on top next to a group photo of police officers in dress uniforms. A half dozen framed certificates and awards hung on the wall. He currently worked part time as an investigator for a private company. The computer where Oakie sat was covered with a pillowcase on which was embroidered "DO NOT TOUCH." The pillowcase, apparently, was a gift from a company secretary who understood Oakie's temperament.

Mark and Linda checked the sinks for leaks again, then departed.

The last apartment was rented by a young couple from the wilds of Chicago. The two left a big city to live near another big city. Eddie was a short order cook, and Eva was a waitress. They seemed especially nervous about Linda and Mark looking about their place. They spoke in short, muted sentences. Eddie blinked his eyes rapidly and constantly licked his lips. Linda could hardly tell they were both 19 years old. They did their short walk-through and Linda poked her flashlight under the sinks and into closet corners for termite damage.

Mark and Linda, satisfied with the interior inspection, left for his office to write up the necessary paperwork.

* * *

WITHIN THREE WEEKS, THE ESCROW CLOSED, AND LINDA added another property to her portfolio. She planned to use the additional income for a newer car, maybe a Bentley.

Rents came in on time, a positive to be sure. But the property itself was losing value, and that was a massive negative. Trash accumulated in the nearby alley. Linda paid no mind at first, but it continued to be a problem.

One day, she drove the length of the alley. A stooped panhandler tried to wave her down, but she ignored him. Later, she saw another fellow in the alley who appeared to be counting something in his palm. She looked closer, and caught a better glimpse of a grimy, wild-haired man. He stared as he babbled, poking a finger into his palm. Linda shuddered at the sight.

At the other end of the alley, toward the next street, a camp had grown from a cardboard lean-to, braced by rocks and discarded junk, into a shanty town with tents and shopping carts. Useless items littered the place. *Something must be done.*

After returning home, Linda called the City Code Enforcement. Some man told her that the law required the homeless to be notified and given due process before they were moved—in other words, there must be an eviction process. Linda hung up the phone, shaking her head in dismay at the bureaucratic nonsense.

* * *

ONE FOGGY MORNING, AFTER COLLECTING RENTS, LINDA decided to check out the alley near the camp. She saw what looked like a fire ring made from rocks and bricks, charred debris, and soot at its center. Beer cans and newspapers were scattered about. Empty pill bottles decorated the area like marigolds.

Looking around, Linda asked herself why the bums couldn't just die from disease or an overdose. A strong smell floated on the breeze. Smoke. The roar of a fire engine screamed, the pitch of its siren growing louder as it raced by.

With that, Linda recalled a name... the one she heard from kids on the street. Dumpster Dan.

The homeless camp did not help Linda's investment. The neighborhood was changing for the worse. One day, as Linda drove along, a tattooed kid was chased from a convenience store. He ran into the street. She braked, narrowly missing the boy. The homeless condition took over neighborhoods one street at a time, she knew. People left to live in better areas; moms stopped letting their kids walk outside alone. A school bus stop moved to another, better street corner.

So many useless people living as panhandlers, even thieves. How else could they get drug money? Later at home, discouraged, Linda poured herself some wine.

She watched the TV news before dinner. A report from a beach resort town said that mail could not be delivered to some homes due to aggressive street people who threatened letter carriers. Drugs were used openly. Spent needles littered people's yards. Sidewalks became public toilets.

Crime in the area had increased. A sheriff's deputy, during an interview, explained that the department does its best to control the problem of drug abuse and crime, but that law enforcement can't be everywhere at once. Also, the mentally ill cannot be forced to seek treatment, and many of these people had severe emotional problems.

Linda poured another drink as she remembered her husband, Benny. She could hear his voice in her head saying that the root of all evil was the lack of money. The more she worried about her problem, the more she thought of how much money she was losing on her new fourplex.

How can the homeless camp be done away with? Eviction? Out of the question. Social Service? It just encourages them to look for handouts. City Council intervention? A waste of time. Then another thought occurred to her: *what about ... chasing them away?*

She snorted, leaning forward as some of her wine dripped from her nose. Then a determined, cold look crossed her face. She twirled the wine glass in her fingers. *Someone could poison them all.* Rising from the couch, she said, "What am I thinking?"

But after another drink, the attitude had taken root in her mind: *they're like pigeons... if you feed one, a hundred more show up!*

She tottered to the kitchen to defrost filet mignon for dinner. Ate, cleaned up. Turned out the lights. Off to bed. As she nestled under the covers and closed her eyes, she saw Benny in heaven, grinning.

★ ★ ★

By EARLY MORNING, LINDA REVIEWED HER BANK accounts as last night's idea crystallized.

After a breakfast of poached eggs, toast, sliced tomatoes, and with a second cup of coffee, she wondered about having someone threaten and chase the bums away. There must be people who would do that. And she could pay for them! It would be just another... investment.

Suddenly, she said aloud, "Buddy the Actor!" Amy's ex-boyfriend. He loved being a joker. Always quite the character when he visited Linda's home. He might think it fun to confront squatters. A little "leaning" on them might persuade them to relocate to the other side of town.

Would Buddy care to go along? Only if he thought it worthwhile.

Linda recalled a short film he made for a college class about the reaction of mail carriers to the sound of a pack of dogs attacking people on the street. The comic film showed real mail carriers running for their lives. It won a film class award—and a reprimand from the college president.

She thumbed through some notes she found in a drawer, and found Buddy's address and phone number. She wondered if he still lived with young students north of town. As she inhaled deeply, she called the number.

A groggy voice answered, "Hello?"

"Um yes, I'm calling for Buddy Brandon. My daughter Amy was in school with him, and I was wondering if I could talk to him."

The man cleared his throat. "Oh yeah! I remember Amy. Nice girl, how is she doing?"

"Fine, she lives in Portland, Oregon now."

"Oh. Well, let me see if I can find the Bud Man. Hold on." Buddy's roommate walked to a sliding glass door. He opened it to find Buddy sitting on the patio smoking a cigar. "Hey! Remember that girl, Amy, you used to go out with? Her mother's on the phone... said she wants to talk to you."

Buddy's jaw dropped, face now drained. He spit up his beer as he leaned forward. "What does she want? Is something wrong?"

"I don't know. Come and answer the phone. I'm expecting my own call!"

"Okay, take it easy, Mick. Don't be such a damn hot head, and calm down already."

Buddy ran his fingers through his short blonde hair, leaned his weight forward, then rose to his full height. He scratched his overgrown belly, and stepped through the house to the phone.

"Well, hello, Ms. Landers. This is a surprise. How are you? How's Amy doing?

"She's doing fine, living in Portland now."

"Oh, good! That's a beautiful city, I spent one summer there." Gripping his tattered robe at his chest, he waited with apprehension for Landers to say, "She's pregnant, you bastard!" How would he respond to that? He heard a whispering voice in his head: *just tell her you had nothing to do with it.*

Silence filled the space between them for what seemed too long for a normal break in conversation. Buddy took a breath and asked, "Why the call today, Ms. Landers? Do you need help with something?"

"As matter of fact I do, Buddy. I'm wondering if you can help me with a creative project I'm considering."

Creative project sounded good. Interesting. "What does it involve?" He smiled with relief, then leaned against the wall.

"Let's get together and talk at lunch tomorrow. Or if you're available, at dinner? Would that be okay?"

Buddy asked, "Just for dinner… right Ms. Landers?" His ego wanted to make sure she was not hitting on him.

"Yes, of course. Do you recall where I live? We can meet here, then decide where to go."

"Yeah, fine. What time?"

"Stop by at seven."

"Okay, see you then."

ANYTHING BUT A DIRECT HIT

★ ★ ★

BUDDY RODE TO LINDA'S HOME ON HIS HARLEY Davidson Iron 883. He parked in the driveway, dismounted, then removed his helmet. Linda greeted him at the door. "Welcome, Buddy. It has been some time, hasn't it?"

As he entered the doorway, Buddy extended a hand. Linda ignored it, giving him a full hug instead. "Come in, have a seat." She took his light brown suede coat. "You know, I thought we could have dinner here. We can talk as long as we like, privately."

"Oh, that's fine." Buddy, half smiling, looked toward photos of Amy and Benny on a sandalwood table. "Looking good! So, Amy's in Portland. How is she spending her time up there, if I may ask?"

"She volunteers at some kind of mission that gives away food and clothing. Nothing wrong with that, but it doesn't help anyone. I think it just perpetuates a problem." Linda guided Buddy to the large dining room. "Have a seat at my new Rosewood table. I had it shipped from New Mexico. Would you like some wine?"

"Yeah, just the clear one. You know…uhh…"

She cocked her head. "White wine?"

"Yeah, that's it."

"Okay… be right back."

Linda returned with two large wine glasses. She poured from a bottle of Chardonnay. "This is good stuff," she said, filling both glasses. "Hints of vanilla and spice." An appliance pinged from the kitchen. She emptied her glass. "Be right back."

She returned with a tray of hanger steak with pineapple ginger soy sauce, rice and spinach. "Serve yourself, Buddy. I remember how much you like beef." She smiled coyly.

"Ms. Landers, you didn't have to go through all this trouble." Buddy's eyes brightened as he savored the platter. He picked up his plate, then stopped. "You first ma'am."

"Go ahead, Buddy, and call me Linda."

Buddy drained his glass, enjoying himself and her attention. Linda refilled the glass. "I need to ask, Ms... I mean *Linda*, just what is the project you wanted to talk about?"

She tilted her head back to stretch her neck, and said, "You know I own some rental properties in town," she poured herself another glass, "and I love the income. It gives me a lifestyle I enjoy." She took a sip. "But sometimes things get in the way of business that have to be dealt with."

Buddy, enjoying the meal, raised his eyebrows.

"A number of unemployed *squatters*, as I call them, have parked themselves and their tents and sleeping bags on streets and alleys near one of my best properties. That kind of thing lowers property values, leading to what is called a *distressed area*."

"Yeah, the problem's growing all over." Buddy served himself more dinner. "But how do you get rid of these poor people?"

"They should be told to leave, straight up!" Linda hissed. "There's no reason they should be allowed to ruin the landscape." She leaned closer to him. "Buddy, I need someone to protect me, to protect us all."

"What do you mean?" Buddy stroked his temple.

"Well, I'm wondering if you would go with me to where they've set up a squatters camp and tell them to leave... to go somewhere else."

Buddy crinkled his brow, leaning back. "Oh, I don't know. I don't think they'll leave just because you tell 'em to." He raised his empty glass and Linda poured him another. "You'd have to be kinda forceful with 'em."

"That's what I'm saying, Buddy," she whispered. "Will you help me?"

"Well, I…" He glanced at the table, then around the room, and returned his gaze to Linda. "Well I could, but maybe I could just go do it by myself. That way you wouldn't be involved, right?"

"That would be great Buddy. Let me get my checkbook!"

"What? Wait. What for? You don't have to pay me for anything, Ms. Landers."

"Linda, Buddy, Linda."

They reached an agreement, then the two enjoyed a dessert of peach swirl cake with ice cream. Linda served coffee and said goodbye at the door. She gave Buddy a massive hug. She wanted to kiss him, too, but stopped herself.

On the way home, Buddy figured out how to do what he had agreed to. He'd ask his roommate, Mick, to be a part of the plan. Mick would agree, since he owed a share of the rent. *Too easy…*

"I don't know if I like this," Mick said. "What's in it for me?" Buddy set a calendar on the table in front of him. "I'll forgive half the rent you owe from last month if you go along." Buddy cracked open a beer bottle. "It could be fun. We'll wear masks." He envisioned turning loudmouth Mick loose on the street.

Mick finally agreed.

★ ★ ★

LATE SATURDAY NIGHT, AFTER SPENDING TIME AT A LOCAL bar, Buddy and Mick drove to the camp that Linda described. They rode up in Mick's huge Tundra pickup truck, and pulled black surgical masks over their faces. They hopped out next to a row of tarp-covered shopping carts, boxes and torn tents.

"What are you guys doin' here?" Mick shouted, giving a brassy performance. "This is private property. You can't just pile crap all over!"

Tattered blankets and cardboard stirred among the piles of debris, as if the entire camp itself came alive. A voice drifted from inside one of the tents, muttering, "We're not hurtin' anybody. Go away!"

Another voice echoed, "There's laws against harassment, ya know."

Another joined in. "We just wanna live free."

Buddy responded, "Yeah, well go live free somewhere else." He puffed his cigar. "There are kids walkin' to school through here. They shouldn't have to step through all this mess!"

Mick rummaged through a nearby shopping cart. "What's in here? Drugs? Stuff you stole?" He pulled his hand out when it touched something wet.

A man stood from his cardboard covered body. "Hands off! That's just my stuff."

"Well get it outta here. It stinks!" Mick eyed the man up and down.

Buddy figured the message had been sent and gave his farewell. "You all had better be gone by tomorrow or we'll be back with our friends! And you don't want that, trust me."

Back in the truck, the two looked at each other. Mick said, "I need a drink."

Without warning, something smashed into the rear of the truck. Mick jumped out to see a plastic jug, half-filled with urine, tumbling to a stop on the street. He picked it up, then threw it back toward the tents. Charging into the camp, grunting like a bear, he picked up the shopping cart and threw it into a nearby tent. He ran through the site, scattering what he could grab. Shouts and yelling rose from all quarters.

He took off back to his truck. "That'll fix em', Buddy." Mick started the engine. The two burned rubber, squealing away.

"Well, what did you do now?" Buddy's cigar smoke filled the cab. "I hope they don't call the cops. Most of those people don't have cell phones, you know, but they might."

"Fine, the cops will see the mess and move them out."

★ ★ ★

TWO DAYS LATER, LINDA SAT AT HER KITCHEN TABLE reading about a disturbance at a homeless camp. She set her coffee down and saw this was Buddy's work. The story said that two men in a truck ran over the camp and harassed the inhabitants. This was all the police knew, and they continued investigating.

Now what? She didn't tell him to run over anyone. Still, her problem might have been solved.

Her cell rang. It was Mr. West from the fourplex. He told Linda that he'd be moving to a larger place to accommodate himself and his sister, recently arriving from Nevada. Linda responded, "You will be breaking the lease, Mr. West."

"Yes, I know, for as long as the place is empty." He cleared his throat. "But I have an opportunity that I can't ignore." The two agreed on a moving date.

Linda would now have to find new tenants. *Such a morning. What more could happen?* She called Buddy, telling him about the newspaper story. "Buddy, I'm sure you know not to tell anyone about what happened."

"Don't worry, Ms. Landers," he ran the palm of his hand from forehead to his chin, "mum's the word. We shouldn't call each other for a while, okay?"

"Whatever. You call anytime, Buddy! I'll send you something for your trouble."

"No, Ms. Landers, really." Buddy glanced at Mick, sitting across the room, his large hands resting on his knees as he squinted at Buddy.

After ending the call, Linda wrote Buddy a check to keep him loyal in some way. Later, she took it and the rest of her mail to the post office. On the way, she passed the site of the camp, and to her surprise and delight, it had disappeared! Linda was all smiles. She would celebrate later with a fine Chardonnay, but first she had to contact Whitney. When she finally reached him, she appointed his crew to clean up West's empty apartment. The work comprised the usual: inspect for damage, paint, get it ready for new tenants. It was a good time to raise rents, too. And this could make up for what she'd paid Buddy and his roommate.

A week later, as she returned from the market, she saw something and couldn't believe her eyes. A new homeless camp appeared near her own home! That afternoon, Linda received a phone call.

"May I please speak with Linda Landers?"

"Speaking, who's calling?"

"Detective Grady, police department ma'am. Are you the owner of a fourplex residence at 1417 Center Street?"

"Yes. Is there a problem?"

"Hazardous materials were found there, ma'am. Will you please meet me there now? We will explain everything when you get here."

Linda raced to her property in her BMW, a million things tumbling through her mind. On arrival, she saw the fire department there with men dressed in what looked like space suits. Jumping from her car, she saw a uniformed policeman and asked what was happening.

"It looks like a drug lab ma'am. Are you a resident here?"

"I'm the owner." Linda's heart pounded. She crossed her arms over her chest and bent forward.

Detective Grady approached them. "Are you Linda Landers?"

Linda looked up. "Yes. What's going on here?"

"Let's get away from this area and sit in my car."

Grady led her to his vehicle. They sat inside, and he rested his forearm on the steering wheel as he turned toward Linda. "Clandestine production of methamphetamine comprises certain chemicals, including hydrochloric acid, ammonia, ether, pseudoephedrine, and iodine, among others. The production, or "cooking" of the drug, produces a smell something like urine or rotten eggs. Mr. Hardwick discovered the smell and called it in. I believe you know him as Oakie." He studied Linda's face. "Would you like some water or anything?"

She shook her head. "No, thank you. When can I have the place cleaned out?"

Grady reached for a clipboard on the dash. "Well, Ms. Landers, you can't. The residence is being evacuated while the fire department assesses the situation, removes any chemicals, that are extremely poisonous. Then Code Enforcement, after posting the property, determines when and if the property can be used again." He eyed the clipboard. "That may take quite a while, Ms. Landers."

Linda had started the week elated. Now, she felt defeated. "Who was making these drugs? Was it the two guys, Chris and what's his name?"

"No. A young couple." Grady checked his clipboard. "Mr. Edward Solvi and his girlfriend, Eva Healy. They're wanted in Illinois for grand theft." Grady placed the clipboard on the dash. "These two are not very smart. They could've burned the place down or poisoned everyone. Did you vet the tenants before they moved in?"

Linda sighed as she took it all in. "They were already in there when I bought the place."

She watched as fire and code officials tagged the property with notices.

Grady leaned forward, "There was a disturbance in a homeless camp nearby a while back. Do you know anything about that?" He checked his notebook as he spoke. "The reason I ask is that your tenants stated that they thought homeless people might possibly be involved in drug making."

Linda cleared her throat. "No, nothing."

"Okay, well here's my card. Call me for any updates, or if you have any questions."

★ ★ ★

A WEEK LATER, LINDA RECEIVED A PROPERTY TAX BILL for the vacant property. A discussion with county land use revealed that, absent a waiver, she was obligated to pay all taxes due. A waiver could take a full year.

Linda, scheming to rid herself of the homeless, was actually now responsible for more homelessness. Stuck with an apparently useless property, she knew she had to act. There was still insurance on the fourplex. The situation strained her finances and tortured her mind.

She dressed in her oldest clothes, then set out in her Lincoln late at night toward town with road flares she found in the garage. She parked in the alley near the now vacant fourplex. She wore a dirty coat and dark wide-brim hat. She sneaked around the back of the building. She popped open a back door with a screwdriver, then tore away the warning sign pasted on it. Once inside, she shone her small flashlight around. An awful smell made her gag. The floor was gritty. She stepped on a dead rat. *The place can still show a profit*, she said to herself.

After removing a sandpaper cap from one flare, she struck the accelerant tip against it. A torchlike flame sprang to life. She tossed it under a sink near old newspapers and plastic bottles half full with old cleaner. Then she lit others, placing them in kitchen cabinets. *The bums will get blamed for this.* One flare popped as she struck it. Red hot sparks flew out, one touching her face. "Ahhh," she yelled.

As she scrambled out, she slowed as she reached the alley, then peered out from behind bushes. She crept to her car and, once inside, checked her face in the rearview mirror. Black marks stained her cheek. The largest was about the size of a grain of rice.

On the way home, she grit her teeth as she passed the camp near her house. Finally, in her kitchen her heart rate normalized, and she opened her last bottle of expensive Chardonnay in celebration before tending to her face. After downing a glass, she strolled to the bathroom and scrutinized the burn mark. She dabbed Neosporin on the large one, then went to bed, and fell to sleep.

★ ★ ★

NEXT MORNING, AT 10:00 AM, THE PHONE RANG. LINDA had been awake for some time and was catching up on news.

"Hello?"

"This is the city fire department calling for Linda Landers."

"Speaking. What's this about?"

"You are the owner of a fourplex on Center Street?"

"Yes," Linda prepared herself for what she knew would be coming. "Is something wrong?"

"Ms. Landers, there was a fire there last night. We would like you to come to the property while our department is on the scene."

"Oh, my God! What happened?" Linda groaned, "How bad is it?"

"Please come down as soon as possible. Someone will meet you there."

"Oh God! I'll be there right away." Linda pulled on her jeans and a blouse, then washed her face and applied some makeup to cover the burn mark.

Linda arrived at the fourplex and gasped. Half the building was missing. The other half comprised blackened doors, and the windows had been punched out. Hose lines adorned the street. Firemen in yellow hats and coats scurried about. Linda stepped out from her BMW.

"Ms. Landers!" The voice was familiar. "It's me... Detective Grady."

"Oh, Detective Grady! What brings you here? I was expecting a fire marshal or something."

"Well, with the drug lab we found, this place is on our watch list."

As she caught her breath, Linda turned toward the building. "Do you think homeless people accidentally did this? Haven't they been known to light fires in some areas, like this Dumpster Dan guy?" She faced Grady.

"It's possible. We have more work to do with arson investigation." Grady reached into his deep coat pocket and pulled out a plastic bag. "We found this in the back yard and tagged it." A flashlight, with a sticker on it reading "L L".

"This is a pretty nice one. Looks new. This brand retails for around a hundred bucks." He paused. "Do you have any idea how it got here?"

Linda gulped, trying to remain composed. "Maybe it was stolen?" She turned back toward the property. "Can I have a closer look at the damage, Detective Grady?" Without waiting, she stepped over puddles of water and a firehose, toward the sidewalk.

"Hold on, ma'am, not until the scene is cleared. This will take a few days minimum, Ms. Landers, before you can go in."

"Oh, all right then. I suppose I should wait and check with the insurance company..." Linda caught herself, realizing she'd said too much. "Will you keep me informed?"

"Yes, I'll be in touch." Grady put the plastic bag back in his pocket, scrutinizing her face. "Looks like you have something on your cheek."

"Age spots, I suppose." She knew she had to leave. With her best soft voice, she said, "I've never dealt with anything like this. I need to go home and get some rest."

Grady smiled, handed her another card, then stepped closer to the scene. After showing his badge to a fireman he walked up to the wrecked building.

Then, as if remembering something, Grady turned around. "Wait, Ms. Landers!" He ran back to her driver's side door. Linda opened her window. "I should tell you about one of your former tenants... Eva Healy." Grady leaned toward the window. "She's been released from custody. Her boyfriend claimed he's the one to blame for attempting to make methamphetamine at their apartment. Eva's pretty angry over the arrest—said it's your fault. She's still getting high, no doubt, so just be aware and be careful. You never know what someone like that will do."

"Ok, Detective, I will." Linda drove away. Reaching into her center console, she found some antacid tablets. She said to herself, "I've done it now. Why in hell did I ever put my initials on that flashlight?"

Once at home, Linda schemed on how she would deal with matters, post fire. She searched her files for documents—property title, fire insurance, lawyer's office.

She called her lawyer to explain about the fire and the investigation, along with details of what Detective Grady had said. The lawyer noted that if and until there were any charges, he could do nothing.

She decided to call her daughter, Amy, but all she got was the voice mail. *"Hello, this is Amy, volunteer for Life House. Leave a message after the tone... thank you."*

"Amy, this is your mother calling to see how you're doing. Hope you're well. We can talk later. Bye honey... love you." Linda hung up and walked to her medicine cabinet for some relaxers. Then, she strolled to the kitchen for some sushi and port wine. After a quick meal, she collapsed in bed and slept.

★ ★ ★

NEXT MORNING, BEFORE DAYLIGHT, LINDA JUMPED awake at the sound of her phone. She reached over to the bedside table. "Hello?"

"Hello, Mom. Sorry I missed your call yesterday. How are you doing?"

"Well, I'm alright. There was a fire at some apartments I own. Probably started by some homeless trespassers."

"Oh, man! Was anyone hurt?"

Linda cleared her throat. "No, just my pocketbook." Linda laughed. "But it can take a hit."

"Okay... well, I'm working at a bank and doing my thing at Life House for the Homeless. No boyfriend yet."

"You keep on with the bank. That's where the money is."

Unsurprised by her mother's tone, Amy giggled. "Well, Mom, I need to get to work," she tugged at the collar of her blouse. "Please let me know if you need anything."

"Okay honey, love you."

Linda needed to clear her mind. Shopping, hairdo, nails, a facial to clear her almost singed complexion... that would fix her up. As she gazed in her bathroom mirror, she said, "I'm not worried about anything."

After a shower, she dressed for the trip to the mall. She stepped downstairs to her garage, then opened the outside door. She passed the old Lincoln and put her hand on the door to her BMW.

A voice from the shadows shook her. "Good day, Ms. Landers."

"Oh," she said, startled, "you shouldn't sneak up like that."

It was Detective Grady. "I'm sorry, ma'am... didn't mean to startle you. I just stopped by to ask some questions. He took a notebook from inside his coat. "I see you have a vintage '96 Lincoln."

"Yes, it's right here." She moved her hand to cover her face. "So, what's the deal, Detective? What's going on?"

"Umm... well, a car like this was seen parked near your property at the time of the fire. This model is distinctive, I'm sure you know."

Linda fidgeted. "So what are you saying? Listen, I'd never do harm to my own property." Sweat trickled along her collar. "I need to get going. May we please talk some other time?"

The detective eyed her closely. "Recall that this was found at the scene." He held up a pocket-sized photo of the flashlight. "It has your initials on it."

"Those could be anybody's initials. Look, you can't just come over here without calling first!"

"Calm down, ma'am. We would like you to come to the office for an interview."

"Talk to my lawyer." Linda stepped into her car. "I'm leaving now."

Grady strolled to his car. He left to complete paperwork and, more importantly, to meet with the District Attorney.

He found the DA in his office and gave him a quick overview of the police investigation. The District Attorney responded, "Arson is one of the easiest crimes to get away with. The arrest rate is about 20% with convictions less than that." He leaned back in his chair staring at Grady, twirling a pen in his fingers. "So, Grady, show me what you've got."

★ ★ ★

THIS IS WHY LINDA LANDERS WAS IN CRIMINAL COURT awaiting a verdict in her case.

At last, the door to the jury room opened, and a burly bailiff guided the jury members in. The judge took his seat, reviewed the papers, and asked, "Madam Foreperson, has the jury reached a verdict?"

A woman wearing a thick black wig, glasses, and dressed in a colorful print, stood up. "Yes, we have, your Honor."

The judge straightened her back. "The defendant will now stand as the verdict is read." Then, turning to the jury foreperson, she said, "Please read the verdict."

The foreperson cleared her throat. "Based on the evidence presented at trial, on the count of arson in the first degree, we find the defendant... not guilty."

A buzz rose from the gallery.

"On the count of attempted insurance fraud, we find the defendant... not guilty."

Linda hugged her attorney, and whispered in his ear, "Let's get some champagne." On her way out of the court room, she passed Amy and Buddy sitting in the gallery, near the aisle. They stared at her, expressionless. Linda patted Amy on the shoulder, then walked out of the court room. She then continued through the hallway toward the exit, swinging a new Gucci handbag.

She could not know that, at the bottom of the courthouse steps, Eva Healy, wearing a black hoodie, fingered a sharp filet knife and waited.

ABOUT THE AUTHOR

Jerry Garces, a veteran, lives in California with his wife Shirley and their little dog, Cleo. He spent his working years as a newsboy, laborer, fry cook, machinist, educator, real estate agent, firefighter, and office professional. He once made a solo parachute jump from 2800 feet at a sky diving school when he was just 17. The jump was allowed based on a permission slip written by his mother to an instructor.

Made in the USA
Las Vegas, NV
15 August 2023